FIGHTER'S FOREVER

Crown MMA Romance: The Outsiders

A. RIVERS

Prologue

TONY

The scent of menthol and sweat is heavy in the locker room as I test the firmness of the wraps my coach, Seth Isles, has secured around my hands.

"All good?" he asks.

"Feels like it." I stand and shadowbox a few times. "Yeah."

He claps me on the shoulder and turns to Leo, one of my training buddies, who's hovering nearby. Leo doesn't have a fight tonight, so he's here to support me. "Leo, will you take him through some pads while I do Gabe's hands?"

"Got it." Leo nods and grabs a couple of focus mitts from a bench along the side of the room.

We find a small area out of the way, and Leo holds the mitts up and calls for various strikes. I throw them, keeping the impact relatively soft. Right before a fight isn't the time for hard training. I just need to warm up my body and get my muscle memory firing. At the end of the day, less than half of the things I do during a fight are conscious choices.

For the most part, my body simply repeats movements I've drilled into it thousands of times before.

"Tony!" a woman calls over the murmured background noise.

I wince. I'd recognize that voice anywhere, and while I'm usually glad to see her, now isn't the best time for my mother to make an appearance. I need to be fully focused, not distracted by the chaos that always follows in her wake. Gia Romano may be vivacious and charming, but she's also a hurricane in human form. And where she goes, my sisters are sure to follow. They haven't yet realized the effect five loud and opinionated Romano women have on their surroundings.

"Hi, Mamma," I say, indicating to Leo that I'll be back in a moment. I greet her with a kiss on the cheek. But then I come to a stop because it isn't one of my sisters standing behind her. It's a man. A tall, handsome devil who's gazing at her with adoration. That in itself is nothing new. Much as I'd prefer not to admit it, Mom is a beautiful woman. My friends used to tease me about it mercilessly. But what's different is the way she glances up at him and her expression softens. She's always been a cynic when it comes to romance. After her roller-coaster marriage to my father ended in disaster, she never gave her heart away fully again. But now something seems to have changed, and I don't like it. Who is this guy, and why is he here?

"Are you going to introduce us?" I ask.

"This is Kevin." She grabs his hand and takes a deep breath. "My fiancée."

My stomach drops. "Your *what*?"

She shows me her left hand, upon which a massive diamond ring sparkles. I have no idea how I didn't notice it previously because now it's all I can see. I look from the ring to Kevin's reserved but proud face to Mom's own glowing smile.

"We're getting married! Isn't it wonderful?"

"Are you serious?" All I can think is that she's playing some kind of joke, but much as I wish that were true, her level of excitement tells me she's not. My mother, who vowed never to be a fool for love again, has decided to remarry. And I hadn't even met her husband-to-be until now. In a strange way, it's predictable in its unpredictability. Mom has always been the type of person to act first and deal with the consequences later. "How long have you been seeing each other?"

She pulls a face, her eyes telling me all I need to know. Their relationship is still new. Once again, she's rushing fearlessly into something that's bound to cause trouble. "Only a couple of months, but when you know, you know." She bounces happily—quite a feat in the heels she's wearing. "We don't want to waste any time."

I narrow my eyes at Kevin, who has remained silent. I want to demand to know what his game is. I refuse to see Mom get hurt again. It was bad enough the first time around. I was only twelve, but I remember it vividly. The tears, the screaming, the way she became a wreck of a human. Now here she is, lining up to do it again.

"Nice to meet you, Kevin," I grit out, barely able to handle the nicety. Her actions, I understand. She's impulsive. Reckless. But why the hell would he propose to someone after only a few weeks? "I'm Tony."

For the first time, Kevin smiles. He reaches for my hand and shakes it firmly. "Gia has told me a lot about you. It's a pleasure to finally meet you."

He's a little too smooth. I don't like it.

"It's a shame I haven't heard anything about you." I can't resist the barb. My emotions are in turmoil. I can't believe Mom would spring something like this on me right before a fight. I need my head to be clear, but now, any thoughts of my fight plan are long gone, smothered by questions and concerns.

"I'm sure we'll have plenty of opportunities to remedy that." He nods firmly, as though the matter is settled.

"Well." Mom claps her hands. "That's our exciting news. I was going to wait to share it until after, but I wanted to see you." She smiles warmly, and I melt a tiny bit in response. Her enthusiasm for life is hard to resist. "You know how I like to wish you luck ahead of time."

"Come here." I scoop her into a hug, eyeballing Kevin over her shoulder.

When I let her go, she pats my cheek. "We'll see you later, Antonio. Go do what you do best."

I force a smile. "Ciao, Mamma."

They leave together, and I return to where Leo had been, only to find Seth has replaced him.

"Who was that?" Seth asks, nodding toward the exit.

"Mom's new fiancée," I reply.

His brow furrows in surprise. "I didn't know she was even dating someone."

"Neither did I," I say meaningfully.

"Oh."

We don't mention it again, but I can't get the situation out of my head. It has catastrophe written all over it, and I'll be the one left trying to pick up the pieces. That's always how it is when the Romano women get their hearts broken.

Seth checks my supplies. When an usher comes for us, Seth and Leo accompany me into the stadium. I raise my arms as the audience cheers, hoping if I put on a good game face, perhaps I'll be able to trick my mind into focusing on what comes next. I spot a couple of pretty brunettes sitting near the aisle and wink at them. One of them blows me a kiss. Usually I'd be thinking about how I could find her later, but instead, she vanishes from my mind the second I look away.

That's how I know I'm in a bad place.

I'm distracted. Something I never should be going into a fight.

We enter the cage, and the umpire checks my mouth guard and wraps. I stand to one side of the octagon and my opponent, a barrel of a man, stands opposite. They summon us to the center, but I don't hear the umpire's usual spiel about safety blah blah blah because my mind won't settle.

I return to my side and wait until the buzzer signals the start of the first round.

My opponent moves forward, circling around me. I throw the first punch, but it isn't as crisp as I'd like, and he evades and throws a counterstrike. My brain struggles to process his actions, and the fact that responses have been drilled into me repetitively is the only thing that saves me from getting flattened immediately.

Get your head in the fight.

I try to read his cues. To see what he's going to do next. But then I catch sight of Mom and Kevin behind him, in the front row seats they must have reserved.

Next thing I know, I'm on the mats, in a left side arm bar. The pressure on my upper arm and shoulder is intense. I struggle to break free, but he's pinned me well. I can't see a way out, but I don't want to give up either. Not so soon into the fight. It's fucking embarrassing.

"Tap out," he growls in my ear, deepening the pressure.

I refuse.

He tightens the hold again. Sharp pain explodes in my shoulder, and I gasp, my vision swimming.

That isn't normal.

Something seriously bad just happened.

I think I might be sick.

My shoulder throbs, nausea churning in my gut, and reluctantly, I reach out and tap the mat. When my opponent releases me, I clutch my arm and gaze sightlessly at the ceiling, hoping I haven't just lost more than a single fight. This feels like the kind of injury that could ruin my career.

Chapter One

TONY

After one day of being coddled by my entire family—who have seen fit to invite themselves to move into my home temporarily—I'm yearning to be alone to suffer in silence. First, the Romano women descended on the hospital *en masse* after my injury, and then when I was discharged after an MRI scan confirmed my rotator cuff tendon had been torn, they formed a protective shield around me and haven't given me a chance to breathe since.

My family means well. They're doing their best to prevent me from dwelling on how this could derail my career. According to the doctor I spoke to last night, and the physiotherapist who visited earlier today, I shouldn't train for at least two months. After that, if the tendon is healing well, I'll be able to have a staged return to work. If it isn't, then I might need surgery, which would mean several more months of recovery. Either way, it throws my training schedule out of whack. Best-case scenario, by the time I build myself up to fighting fitness, I will have been out of action for five or six months. That's a lot of time in my world.

And what do I have without training? My life has been MMA and parties for ten years.

"Tony," Stella says, bustling into the room. She, Mom, and my other sisters have been taking turns to sit with me as though I'm an invalid while the rest of them gossip in the kitchen. Mia just left, so I knew one of the others would be here within a couple of minutes. I'm just glad it's Stella and she's come alone.

"What kind of Italian man has nothing more than milk, eggs, and protein powder in his kitchen?" She throws her hands up in disgust. "It's a travesty. How am I supposed to cook for you when I have nothing to work with?"

I sigh. "Nobody asked you to cook, Stel. If we need food, I can order in. There are a couple of good places nearby that deliver."

"Pah!" She glares at me, her hands going to her slim hips. "Don't insult me like that. You need real food to build your strength up. I'll send Bianca to the shop."

I'm sure Bianca, the youngest of my sisters—and the only one who isn't divorced—won't appreciate being sent on an errand. She constantly has a bee in her bonnet about her older sisters bossing her around. "I appreciate you wanting to look after me, but you know B will hate having to go on her own."

She purses her lips. "You're right. Mia can go with her. It's not her turn to—" She breaks off and glances at me guiltily.

Despite myself, I chuckle. "It's okay, Stel. I know you guys have a roster." I pat the sofa beside me. "Sit for a moment." It's the first time I've had a chance to get her alone. While all the Romano women are opinionated, Stella, in particular, never holds back. I want her thoughts on Mom's new fiancée. With a huff, Stella lowers herself onto the cushion and crosses her long legs. "What do you think of Kevin?"

She cocks her head. "He's a bit boring if you ask me. Doesn't have any passion." She emphasizes this with her hands. "He reminds me of Mr. Black from high school math class. Was he still there when you were in school?"

I nod, knowing exactly who she means. The guy had been an institution. He taught every Romano child, despite the fact there are twelve years between us. At thirty, I'm the youngest. Adele is the oldest, followed by Stella, Mia, and Bianca.

"But do you think there's anything off about him?" I prompt.

"Who, Kevin?" She taps a finger to her chin. "No, I don't think so. He seems like the kind of person who files his taxes on time, never gets speeding tickets, and has a pair of underwear for each day of the week."

I cringe because I don't want to think about Kevin's underwear. "Did you meet him before they got engaged?"

"No, but she mentioned him a few times." She reaches over and rests a hand on my knee. It's intended to be reassuring, but I feel like I'm going to burst out of my skin. "Asking her to marry him is probably the craziest thing that man has done in his life, which must mean he really loves her. Don't worry so much."

I'm not sure I agree. I'm concerned they're jumping into this too quickly and not thinking things through—something that never ends well when it comes to Mom. I open my mouth to say as much, but the door swings inward, and the rest of the family enters the room. Behind them is Kevin. I take a moment to glare at him while he's not looking, quickly schooling my features as his eyes find mine.

"Sorry last night didn't go the way you wanted," Kevin says, his mouth tilting sympathetically. "Gia told me you've torn your rotator cuff. I did that playing baseball in college. Took forever to heal. If you need any suggestions for stretches or exercises, I'm your man."

Took forever to heal. Exactly what I want to hear.

"Thanks." I rest my head against the back of the couch while my mother and sisters bicker over what they're going to cook for dinner and who'll be in charge of the kitchen. I sigh. They're all excellent cooks, but their behavior right now is the reason I stayed out of their way growing up. The last thing they need is another person getting involved.

My phone vibrates, and I surreptitiously slip it from my pocket and study the screen. It's a message from Leo.

Leo: *How are you doing?*

I type out a response.

Tony: *Shoulder aches. Got a headache coming on. My family is all in one room and you know how that usually ends.*

Leo: *Oh damn. Need a rescue?*

Tony: *No, but thanks anyway. I doubt they'll let me leave. They're in overprotective mode. It's sweet but intense.*

A few moments later, my phone rings. I answer immediately, assuming it's Leo.

"Hey, Tony." It's Gabe. One of the other fighters at the gym. "Leo said you're going crazy at home."

"Just a little," I murmur, glancing at my relatives, who have stopped arguing to listen in. "Snoops," I mouth. Stella rolls her eyes, and Mom raises one brow dangerously. I look away. "What's up?"

"You know Sydney and I have a cottage on Cape Cod?" he asks.

"Yeah," I reply, not sure where the conversation is going.

"You're welcome to use it as a getaway. Hide out there for a few weeks while you rest." He's obviously smiling; I can hear it in his voice. "The ocean air is great for recuperating."

"Wow, thanks for the offer." I never expected anything like this. Mia leans forward, her bangs falling over her face, clearly interested to know what we're talking about. Bianca gives her a little shove, gesturing for her to leave me alone. "I don't know, though. I don't want to be away from the gym for that long."

Gabe makes a sound of understanding. "I get that. But if you're here all the time, you'll only be torturing yourself. You know Seth won't let you join in until you've been cleared by a physiotherapist. You can keep up your base fitness from anywhere, and maybe being away will do you some good."

I nod because he's right. I will find it difficult to watch others train and not join them. And I know my sisters will have already planned to visit me every day for the foreseeable future. I love them, but I need space. Maybe it's not the worst idea.

"I'll think about it," I tell him.

"Great." He hesitates, then adds, "If you decide not to, you can change your mind any time, but no pressure. It sits there empty for most of the year."

"Thanks." I manage to summon a smile. "I'll be in touch."

We end the call and my mother begins an interrogation, wanting to know exactly who had called and what they wanted. When Kevin chimes in, I pull a face. Perhaps being on the other side of the country is what I need.

———

Lucia

I breathe in the salty air and gaze at the ocean as it laps the sand a few yards from where I'm sitting. Sydney and Gabe's cottage in Provincetown backs onto the beach, with an elevated wooden deck from which I've enjoyed many sunsets over the past two weeks. I met Sydney through my sister-in-law, Tempe, and when Sydney said I could use their cottage while I finish the book I've been trying to write for months, I leaped at the chance. This romance novel is the story of my heart. My chance to break free of a cycle of freelance magazine articles to enter the world of novel publishing. If only I could finish it. But I tore my hero and heroine apart so well that I haven't been able to figure out how to put them back together, and the harder I rack my brain for a solution, the more I fear the entire story is flawed.

I've tried writing at home, at the library, in coffee shops, and practically anywhere I can take my laptop, but it hasn't worked. I was hoping that here, thousands of miles from home, with nothing to distract me, I'd finally be able to write The End. Unfortunately, I haven't had any epiphanies yet. It's been more of the same: staring at my screen, typing a few words, then deleting them. Once or twice I thought I was onto something, but as soon as I tried to grab the story thread and follow it, everything unraveled.

I close my eyes and listen to the sound of the water. Somewhere up the beach, children laugh. I exhale slowly. I still have time. But I'm beginning to lose faith in myself.

Bang!

I shoot to my feet and whirl around to face the glass sliding doors that lead into the house. The sound came from *inside*, I'm sure of it.

But I'm the only one here.

Heart in my throat, I debate whether to investigate or call the police, but that seems like overkill. I'm a strong, capable woman.

There's another clatter, and I flinch. That one definitely came from inside. I look around for something I can use as a weapon and spot a kayak paddle leaning against the rail. I brandish it like a baseball bat as I make my way in, ducking through the entrance so the paddle doesn't hit the doorframe. I tiptoe through the living room and pause at the entrance to the hallway, just out of sight. I position myself to one side of the doorway and raise the paddle, straining to hear anything. There are soft footfalls down the hall. The floor is wooden, so it's easy to follow the intruder's progress. They pause midway along the hall, then resume. They're nearly at the living room. The footsteps draw closer and I hold my breath, tense my muscles, ready to strike if needed.

A man appears in the doorway, and I shriek and start to swing the paddle, but then I catch sight of his face. Recognition sets in. But I'm already in motion. I stumble backward to avoid hitting him and trip over the edge of a mat, falling on my ass. The paddle lands on my lap and I give an "oof."

"What the fuck?" Tony stares at me with astonishment, his eyes wide with shock. It takes a moment for him to realize who I am. "Lucia?" He glances from me to the paddle. "I hope you weren't planning to attack me with that."

A laugh escapes. "I thought you were a burglar."

His brows draw together. "You thought I was a burglar, and you planned to confront me?"

Put like that, it doesn't sound like the smartest idea.

"Uh, yeah."

He shakes his head in disbelief. His dark brown hair hangs loose around his face and shoulders. Long hair makes some men seem softer, but not Tony. With his chiseled features and muscular body, all it does is make him seem more like a gladiator… or a pirate.

Hmm, I could write a romance novel about a pirate. That would be fun. I immediately picture Tony as a swashbuckling hero. Bad idea. I'm attracted to him on the best of days without adding that image. Not that anything could come of it. He's a first-class playboy, and I'm the kind of girl who won't settle for less than happily ever after. No matter how tempting a romp with Mr. Right Now might seem.

I inwardly chastise myself for even thinking of it. It's not as though I'd have the opportunity to engage in a wild fling with Tony, even if I wanted to. He keeps his distance from me. I suspect Mercy and Tempe are to blame for that. They're a bit overprotective.

Tony reaches for me, but then he flinches and swaps hands, offering me his right one instead. Curious. "Here."

"Are you okay?" I ask, eyeing the arm he withdrew.

His lips press together. "Got injured in a fight a few days ago. But it's fine."

"I'm so sorry." I take his hand and let him pull me to my feet. "I hope it's nothing serious." The fact he doesn't answer makes me think it is. "What are you doing here?"

"Me?" he asks, sounding surprised. "Gabe gave me a key and said I could use the cottage to recover in peace and quiet. There's not much of that at home at the moment. He didn't mention you'd be here."

"Oh." I manage not to flinch. He came here wanting to be alone, and he's been landed with me instead. "Maybe Gabe forgot." I dust myself off and sit on the sofa, gesturing for him to join me. "Sydney is letting me use this as a writing retreat to finish a book I'm working on."

His eyes light with interest. "You're writing a book?"

"Yes." My cheeks heat. I'm not about to explain exactly what type of book it is. Knowing him, he'll tease me. Not to be cruel, but because he wouldn't realize it's a sensitive topic.

"That's awesome." He smiles, and it's the first time he's done so since he entered, which is strange. Tony is usually all smiles and charm. "What's it about?"

"Uh. It's a historical novel, set in England." Technically, that's correct. There's no need for him to know it's a regency romance about a duke and an American heiress.

"That must involve a lot of research." He looks around the room, apparently cataloging details. "It's a nice place they've got, isn't it?"

I nod. "It's lovely. But they must have crossed their wires about loaning it out."

"I guess so."

Neither of us speaks for a few moments.

"You're welcome to stay," I say to break the silence. "I feel bad for ruining the quiet time you planned, though."

"Don't feel bad; you were here first."

"Are we in kindergarten?"

He chuckles. "Some days, I feel like it."

I study him more closely. He doesn't look great. "Are you sure you're okay?"

"Never better." His tone is brusque. "But I'd hate to intrude on your writing retreat, so I'll grab my bag and find somewhere else to go. I'm sure there are other places to stay around here."

"Don't be silly," I reply before thinking it through. "There's no reason we can't both stay. Especially when you flew all the way here. There are two bedrooms, and I'm so quiet you'll hardly know I'm around."

He hesitates. I can tell he's unsure, and for a moment I hope he'll decide to leave. Honestly, I don't know what I was thinking when I opened my big mouth. I don't want to be stuck living with the most gorgeous man I've ever met— especially not when he's off limits. But I can manage, right? Perhaps it will motivate me to write faster. Besides, he clearly needs rest and relaxation. He's wound tighter than I've ever seen him, and he's spent the day traveling, which won't have helped.

"Okay," he relents. "If you're sure."

"I am." Kind of.

His lips lift at the edges. "Then I'll stay. I'll be in my room for most of the night, though. I'm exhausted."

"Fair enough. Let me show you to the main bedroom. I'm using the spare one, but Sydney said it was fine to use either."

"Thanks." He follows behind as I give him a quick tour of the house, and then he stays in the large ocean-facing master suite while I return to the deck. The air is starting to cool, so it isn't long before I head to the kitchen to prepare dinner for two.

Chapter Two

Tony

I don't know what I did to deserve such a karmic kick in the balls. Everything had been looking up. When I'd gotten on a plane to fly to Massachusetts, I'd been excited, but with one surprise, my excitement has been wiped out. Of all the people to be here, why does it have to be her? Lucia Caruso is the one woman I want most, and the one I can't have.

When I met her at the hospital after Tempe—her sister-in-law and my training buddy—gave birth, I was captivated by her beautiful smile, inky black hair, and compact curves. But then I'd caught sight of her unique eyes—the palest shade of blue and a perfect match for her brother's—and realized who she was. I'd known instantly I couldn't go there. According to Tempe, Lucia wants two point five kids and a white picket fence, whereas I never intend to have a long-term relationship. I've seen the devastation they cause.

I flop onto the bed and wince as pain jolts through me.

This goddamn injury.

I've hardly been able to sleep because I can't put my

weight on my shoulder, and when I lie on the opposite side, it hurts like a bitch because of the way my arm hangs across my body. Carefully, I ease it through some basic movements and gentle stretches the physiotherapist recommended. My eyes tear up as the pain worsens, and I wonder whether to continue or stop. It's hard to know how much movement it needs versus what's going to aggravate it. In the end, I stop and close my eyes, reveling in the silence. Even though Lucia is nearby, I can't hear her at all. The only noise is that of the ocean. Perhaps I haven't got the solitude I wanted, but at least it's peaceful.

I draw in a deep breath and release it, picturing my problems floating away on the exhalation. It's a meditation technique Bianca taught me. Sometimes it works, but right now it's too hard to focus.

I hold the image as my chest rises and falls. Rises and falls.

A knock on the door summons me to the present. I'd hoped Lucia might leave me alone to get my thoughts in order, but it would seem not.

I answer the door. "Hey."

Her gaze catches on my chest, then slowly rises to my face, her cheeks turning pink. God, I wish I could step closer, pull her against my body, and investigate the attraction I see written all over her, but I don't. I'm not the guy who leads women on. I'm better than that.

"I've made chicken for dinner, if you'd like some," she says, her tone friendly but cautious.

"You cooked for me?" I'm touched. Other than my mom and sisters, I can't recall any woman ever cooking me dinner. It's the kind of thing a girlfriend would do, and I don't have girlfriends, as a rule.

Her blush deepens. "I was making some anyway, so I just doubled the portions. If you're not hungry, I can put it in the fridge for later."

"Thank you." *She's so sweet.* "That sounds great."

"Good." She smiles. "I can bring it in here."

I wince. I might have emphasized my desire to be alone a little too much if she doesn't even expect me to sit with her while we eat. "I'll join you. I hadn't thought about food, so thanks. It was nice of you to make extra."

"No problem." She retreats to the living area. I wait until she's gone, then struggle to put a sweater on. It's difficult to get it over my head and manipulate my left arm into the sleeve. I get there eventually, but I'm glad I didn't try to do it in front of her. The last thing I need is for the curvy beauty to view me as an invalid, the same way my sisters do. I don't think my ego could survive.

Lucia is on the sofa in the living room. There's no dining table, so she has her plate on her lap, and mine is sitting on the coffee table. I reach for it, hoping she doesn't notice the way my hand trembles as I sit next to her. I leave a couple of feet of space between us so I'm not tempted to do something stupid, like touch her or kiss her. She's prepared chicken with a sweet-scented golden glaze— perhaps honey—and baked vegetables. I dig in and discover it tastes as good as it looks.

"This is delicious," I tell her.

She beams. "Thanks. I like to cook, but it's always nicer when there's someone else to appreciate it."

"My mom and sisters would agree with that."

She cocks her head. "How many sisters do you have?"

"Four."

Her mouth forms an *O.* "Wow. I can't imagine. It must have been a busy house growing up."

I chuckle at the memory. "Definitely. It was all kinds of crazy."

I scan the room, looking for signs of what she's been up to since she arrived, but she must be a tidy person because there's hardly any indication someone has been living here, except for the open laptop on the coffee table. I nod toward it. "Tell me more about your book."

Her expression pinches. "Oh, you don't want to know the details. I'll bore you to death if you encourage me."

"No, really," I assure her. "It beats talking about my injury, which is all I've gotten to do since last Saturday."

Her lips purse and she looks so anxious I almost tell her not to worry about it. But I want to know. She intrigues me. She always has.

After a moment, she sighs and her shoulders slump. She murmurs something I can barely hear.

"What was that?" I ask, leaning closer.

"It's a romance novel," she repeats more loudly.

"A romance?" *Oh.* "But I thought you said it was an English historical novel."

"It's that too," she says. "But mostly, it's a romance." Her cheeks are the prettiest shade of pink. "I don't like to tell people because they usually tease me or look down their noses at me for it."

"I won't do either," I promise. Learning she's writing a romance novel is a timely reminder that I can't act on my desire for her. It wouldn't be fair when she's clearly a romantic at heart, and I'm the sort of person who'd shatter her illusions. "I think it's impressive you're writing a book, whatever type it is. Not many people would be able to say they've done that." Although I could never read a romance novel myself. I wouldn't be able to suspend my disbelief for long enough to buy into the notion of happily ever after.

She smiles shyly. "Thanks. I'm still not going to tell you the plot, though. I'm working out the kinks, and I don't want to jinx it."

"Fair enough." I fork chicken into my mouth. "I tore my rotator cuff tendon. It's going to take at least a couple of months to heal. Might need surgery, but I hope not."

"I hope not too." Her expression is sympathetic. "That must be scary for you."

I nod but don't say anything more, and she doesn't pry. We finish our meal in relative silence, and I offer to clean up, which I regret as soon as I realize how difficult it's going to be. Fortunately, she disappears into another room, and soon after, I hear the shower start. I'm pleased not to have an audience as I battle to do an everyday task. When I finally finish, I head for the main bedroom, but as I pass the hallway, I catch a glimpse of Lucia's shapely legs as she darts from the bathroom across to her bedroom, wrapped in only a towel. My dick stiffens and I groan. Living with her temporarily is going to be hell.

———

LUCIA

I wake wrapped in a blanket burrito, snug and warm, and smile as the soft light of the morning sun passes through the filmy curtain. I had an amazing sleep, and I'm optimistic for the day ahead. Perhaps I'll have a break-through. I slip from the bed and pad barefoot through the cottage, finding the living area empty. I frown. There's no sign of Tony, and for a moment I'm gripped by the possibility I might have dreamed the whole thing, but then I see the dishes draining on the bench and know he's been here. But even though he must be around, he hasn't left any evidence of his presence in the living room. The door to the master bedroom is ajar, and the bed is empty. He must have gone out.

I shower and put on a summery dress designed by up-and-coming fashionista Camile Hayes. I met Camile once. She's dating a fighter who trains out of the same gym as Tempe and Tony. She seemed nice. A bit quiet, but very sweet. Even if she hadn't been, she'd still be a genius. Her designs flatter the right parts of me and skim over the bits I'd rather no one pay attention to. Not that I'm particularly sensitive about my figure, but I'm what some people might call thick, and I know that's not for everyone.

I sling my handbag over my shoulder and choose a pair of cute flats to wear into town. I went out in heels my first day here and regretted it because I had terrible blisters within a few hours. I lock the door behind me, pausing to wonder whether Tony has a way to get back in, but then I remember he mentioned Gabe giving him a key.

I walk to the bakery, enjoying the warmth of the sun on my arms and legs. Once there, I buy a freshly baked bread roll that's bursting with colorful salad, then give in to temptation and get a mini donut as well.

With a food bag in one hand and a vanilla latte in the other, I stroll back to the cottage. The front door is unlocked, so I let myself in. It crosses my mind that perhaps I should have bought something for Tony, but since he's already been out and about, I'm sure he must have taken care of himself. I kick my shoes off in the hall and follow the sound of muttering into the living room. Tony glances up as I enter, and the muttering abruptly stops. He's scowling, and I'm taken aback by the expression because it's so unfamiliar on his face. My gaze trails down his body and sharpens on the ice pack he's holding to his shoulder.

"Did you hurt yourself?" I ask.

"Nothing major." The pale pallor of his cheeks suggests otherwise, but I don't call him on it. "I went to see a physiotherapist and might have overdone things."

"I thought you'd already been to see a P.T.," I say, confused.

"I did." His words are tight. "But I'll need to see one locally if I'm going to be here for a while, and I wanted a second opinion."

I nod. "Did the second opinion match the first?"

"Yeah." He doesn't sound thrilled about it.

I move past him to the kitchen and set down my haul from the bakery. "Is there anything I can do to help? Get you a painkiller, perhaps?"

I hate to see him hurting. Especially when I know it isn't only physical but mental too. The fear over what this means for his career must be torture.

"No," he snaps, his eyes flashing. "I don't need anyone fussing over me. I had enough of that at home."

Oh. Well, then.

I fall back a step and look away, emotion tightening my throat. I hadn't been expecting his harshness, and I'm not sure how to react. "I'll leave you to it, then."

I start to turn away, intending to grab my breakfast and go out onto the deck, but he reaches toward me, wincing as he jolts his shoulder.

"Wait," he says. "I'm sorry, Luce. That was a really shitty thing to say." He seems contrite, but I don't drop my guard. He makes a pained sound. "I hate being vulnerable, so I acted like a jerk. I'm sorry." He laughs humorlessly. "You're really not seeing me at my best."

I soften because I understand where he's coming from. Tony is like a wounded animal right now. He doesn't want to admit to weakness, so he's lashing out to protect himself. That doesn't make it okay, but I get it.

"Forgiven." I hope he doesn't see my sympathy because I get the feeling it's the last thing he wants. "Just don't make a habit of it."

"I won't," he promises. "Are we good?"

"Yeah." I retrace my steps to the kitchen counter, grab two plates from the cupboard and place my bread roll on one and the donut on the other. "Here." I offer him the donut, sensing he needs it more than I do. "Peace offering?"

His lips pull into a tiny smile. "Are you trying to make me feel even worse for snapping at you?"

"Not at all." I'm glad he seems more relaxed, even if the difference is barely noticeable.

"Thanks." He takes it. "Smells amazing. This is really nice of you."

I wave off his gratitude. "It's a donut, not a gold watch. Don't get carried away." His grin widens, and despite the turmoil lurking behind his eyes, I know we'll be fine. "I'll be on the deck, staring at a blank screen," I tell him. "I'll see you later."

"Good luck with the writing."

I take my breakfast outside, then return to the cottage for my computer. I eat while the laptop fires up and then open a document and review the last few sentences I wrote. Strangely, my fingers are itching to get onto the keyboard, and once they do, the words seem to come easily. The only problem is, they're not completely consistent with the story so far, and the hero seems to bear a startling resemblance to a handsome MMA fighter.

Chapter Three

TONY

A couple of days after I arrive in Provincetown, I'm starting to tire of the silence. I'd looked forward to the opportunity to have some thinking space, but there's only so much moping a guy can do without losing his sanity. I've been keeping up to date with my exercises, and I have another appointment scheduled with the physiotherapist, but other than that, I'm bored. It doesn't make me feel great to admit it, but I'm used to having people around. Training buddies, family, friends. My place is one of those homes where everyone congregates, and sharing a cottage with a woman who spends most of her time focused on her computer is throwing me for a loop.

It's midafternoon, and I've been mulling over my options for the past couple of hours. It's crossed my mind that I could go out tonight and find a pretty distraction at a local bar. Injured shoulder or not, I could show someone a good time, and it would certainly help my ego. But for some reason, the idea of doing that when Lucia is here seems disrespectful. So I reject the thought, just like I have the last half dozen times it's occurred to me. Instead, I decide to investigate the company I already have.

I find Lucia on the deck, where she's been sporadically typing for the past few hours. Her fingers are still now, her eyes flicking over the screen, and she makes a sound of disapproval in the back of her throat.

"Hey," I say as I stand in the open doorway behind her. "How's the story coming?"

"Ugh." She spins around, her nostrils flaring with annoyance. "It's not. It was finally working out, but then I went and got stuck again."

I hide my smile. I shouldn't be pleased by her problems, but I'm hoping they mean she won't be opposed to doing something else for a while. "Do you want to head down to the water? Might do you good to have a break."

She purses her lips, then nods briskly. "Great idea. Just give me a couple of minutes and I'll change into my swimsuit."

Swimsuit?

Damn, I hadn't considered that. I hope whatever she's brought with her covers plenty of skin. The last thing I need is to get the full image of what I want but can't have. Lucia is a forbidden temptation, and she doesn't even know it.

"All right. I'll change too." If she's going to be stripping, there's a good chance I'll need to cool off before the afternoon is done. "Meet back here in five?"

"Perfect." She closes her laptop.

I go to the master bedroom and spend a few minutes thinking unsexy thoughts before changing in time to meet her. She's wearing a colorful wrap that's tied at the back of her neck and falls to mid-thigh, covering anything that might be revealed by a swimsuit. I have a brief moment of gratitude.

"You ready?" she asks.

"Yep." We leave via the glass doors on the deck, and I notice she's taken her laptop inside. I lock them behind us and place the key beneath a small garden ornament, then we walk down the stairs and onto the beach. The sand is warm and soft between my toes. I didn't bother with shoes because they'd only end up full of sand. I scan the ground in front of me, making sure there's nothing sharp to step on, before returning my attention to the waves. They're halfway down the beach, but at high tide, the water nears the cottage. As we get closer to the edge of the surf, the sand firms and becomes damp. I pause just outside reach of the waves, noticing Lucia do the same. Another wave rolls up, stopping short of my toes, and I step forward, flinching at how cold it is on my sun-warmed skin.

"How bad is it?" Lucia asks.

"It's just right," I fib, wondering if she'll buy it.

She dips a toe in and hisses. "Liar!" But she doesn't snatch her foot back. She lowers it fully into the sea and wades deeper, until the water reaches her calves. "I don't think it'll be too bad once we get used to it."

How long does she plan to stay in the water?

The question dies on my lips as she reaches up and undoes her wrap. It flutters around her waist, slowly showing more of her gorgeous skin. She tosses the wrap onto the beach, and I swallow. Hard. She's wearing a one-piece, but it's nothing like any other one-piece I've seen. It displays a ridiculous amount of cleavage while nipping in around her waist and dropping almost all the way to her ass in the back. The fabric seems to mold to her curves, revealing and concealing teasingly. My cock plumps in my trunks, and I stay very still, hoping she won't look down. She gives me a wink and then, with no warning, runs into the water and dives headfirst into the waves. I hurry after because once she surfaces, I run the risk of her seeing my erection.

Fuck, it's cold.

On the upside, my cock can't stand at attention while chilly water is rising up my thighs and cupping my balls.

Thank God.

Lucia breaks through the waves, throwing her head back to get her hair out of her eyes. Water sprays from the long tresses in an arc, and I lose my ability to speak as she opens her beautiful blue eyes and flashes me a mischievous smile.

She's fucking gorgeous.

"Come on, scaredy cat," she calls.

I roll my eyes. I'm too old to be bated by silly dares, aren't I?

But then she turns and dives back in, swimming out a little deeper, and with a sigh, I follow. When she looks at me as though I've made her day, I realize there aren't many places I wouldn't follow her. And that scares me. Because the thoughts I'm having about her aren't fleeting, and I can't offer anything permanent. Forever isn't in the cards for me, which means Lucia isn't for me—no matter how much I may wish she was.

———

LUCIA

Tony Romano in swimming trunks is a sight worthy of being on one of those sexy calendars as Mr. January. He's tall, toned perfection, with a deep V grooving the front of his hips and a bajillion ab muscles popping all over the place. Despite the injury, his shoulders bulge with muscles and his chest is strong with a fine smattering of hair. I want to lick his dark, flat nipples. But I force myself to look away and paddle further from him instead. Not deeper, though, because I don't want him to have to swim with his torn tendon.

I remind myself, once again, Tony isn't interested in me. He has a reputation with women. He doesn't have a type as such—unless stunningly beautiful is a type. Whether they're conventionally pretty, sultry seductresses, or fierce athletes, his dates are undeniably confident and gorgeous.

Then there's me.

A little too curvy, a little too bookish, never quite certain of my place in the world. But then, I guess that's what happens to people who are orphaned at an early age. They never feel like they belong. And no matter how much Mercy says he doesn't blame me for his having to drop out of college to take care of me when our parents died, I never believed him, which meant I was never comfortable with my role in our family.

I was a burden. I'd known it then, and I'd hated it. At first, I'd taken my frustration out on him, but after a while, I'd realized he was doing the best he could, and I feared what might happen to me if he gave up and let them put me into the foster care system. So I did everything I could to make myself less of a problem. I rarely went out with friends. I did the chores, submitted my homework on time, and got straight As in everything except gym class. Being unobtrusive is something I've made myself good at.

Perhaps too good.

I glance back at Tony, who is pacing through the water behind me. For a second, I think I catch a glimpse of heat in his eyes, but it's gone in a flash. Shocked, I stop, and he plows into me, cursing as the movement jars his shoulder. But then our gazes lock, and we both freeze. Now, there's no mistaking his expression.

He wants me.

I shiver, both excited and intimidated by the way his

dark eyes prowl over my features. I wet my lips, and he stares at them, apparently fascinated. I can hardly breathe. I sense we're poised on the edge of a massive change, but I'm not sure I want to make the jump. After all, he's a player, and I'm the girl voted most likely to have a white picket fence.

No, seriously. That was a thing in high school.

I gather a palm full of water and spray it in his face. His mouth drops open, and the heat fades from his eyes, defusing the tension.

"Oh, you're going to get it now," he warns, preparing to retaliate.

I stumble away, tripping over my feet in my haste to escape him. But instead of splashing me, he makes a sudden movement and cries out in pain.

Oh shit.

That's not good.

"Is it your shoulder?"

He nods and grimaces.

"Do we need to get out of the water?" I ask, cursing myself for not being more considerate of his injury. The last thing he needs is to make it worse by playing the fool. "I'm so sorry. I should have thought—"

"It's fine," he growls a little too harshly. "Stop treating me like I'm an invalid. It twinged, that's all."

I glare at him for a moment, understanding he's lashing out because he's feeling vulnerable, but honestly, I don't care what his reasons are. He needs to stop using me as a verbal punching bag when he's upset.

"If you're going to be an ass, we may as well head in." I paddle toward the shore. As soon as I feel sand beneath my toes, I start marching up the beach, shaking water off as I go.

"Sorry!" he calls out from behind me.

I know I'm probably moving too quickly for him to

keep up, but perhaps that's a good thing. I don't feel like listening to him right now.

"Wait, Luce. Hold on."

I can hear him chasing me with all the grace of a lumbering bull, but I don't look back until I feel his hand on my arm. My eyes fly up to his, and they're full of regret. His mouth twists.

"I did it again." He sounds disappointed in himself. "Acted like I was mad at you when I'm really mad at myself. I'm sorry. I'm not used to being anything other than completely in control of myself around beautiful women, and it's bothering me more than I'd like for you to see me this way."

Wait, what?

"Are you trying to butter me up?" I ask skeptically. He looks sincere, but he called me beautiful, and he's never given any indication he thinks that before. Why should I believe him now?

"No. God no." He drags a hand down his face. "Christ, I'm getting this all wrong." He places his hands on my waist. I flinch, tempted to suck in my stomach, but he hardly seems to notice the fact he's touching me. His attention is on our conversation. "You *are* beautiful, Luce." Water drips from his hair over his forehead. "I mean it. I'm not just trying to make you forgive me, okay?"

I shrug, but his grip on my waist tightens.

"Do you believe me?" he demands. "Sei bella. Sei dolce e gentile. Hai dei begli occhi."

You're beautiful. You're sweet and kind. You have beautiful eyes.

I laugh. "Pensi che dirlo in Italiano lo renda più vero?"

Do you think saying it in Italian makes it more true?

He looks at me askance. "I guess I should have known you'd share my heritage with a last name like Caruso." His expression turns mournful. "If I can't whisper sexy Italian nothings, then I have no way of charming you. You'll see right through all my moves."

I roll my eyes, even though I secretly enjoy his teasing. It's far better than the strain of a few moments ago. I take his hand—the right one because I don't want to jostle the left. "Come on, Casanova. I'll make coffee and we can sit on the deck and enjoy the view."

Chapter Four

Tony

By the time a week has passed since my injury, I'm beginning to feel more in control of the surges of emotion that have been coming and going. Frustration has become a constant companion, but I've managed to temper it and not take it out on Lucia. She was right to call me on my douchey behavior, and I'm trying to be better. We've had a truce of sorts since that afternoon on the beach. She doesn't fuss over me or pry for details about how my shoulder is healing, and I ignore any urge to protect myself by being a jerk.

Instead, I distract myself with useful tasks like getting in the laundry. That's what I'm currently doing. I knew it would be tricky when I started, but I won't let it get the better of me. I use my right arm to retrieve a pair of shorts that are hanging on the wire strung along the side of the cottage. I remove a peg from a T-shirt with that same hand and then remove the other peg. I'm not bothering to use my left arm because I can't raise it above my shoulder yet, so it would be another exercise in frustration.

Unfortunately, one-handed, I'm making slow progress.

I curse as I fumble with a peg and drop it. I want to stomp on the damn thing, but I close my eyes and draw in a long, even breath.

It's okay. My body needs time to recover. I'm taking care of myself so I can return to fighting sooner.

I've begun mentally reframing the situation when I sense myself getting angry. It's something I've picked up from Lucia, who seems to see the bright side in everything. While I don't need her acting like my therapist, I can acknowledge there are a few things I could learn from the way she approaches life.

I collect the peg from the ground and move on to a skirt of Lucia's. It feels oddly domestic, the way we're sharing everyday things like laundry duty. It's not something I ever expected. After another fifteen minutes, I've finished, and I awkwardly tuck the washing basket under my right arm and head inside. I drop it on the living room floor and decide to fold it later. For now, it's time to prepare to watch Devon's fight, which will be streamed live from the arena.

Devon is another of my training buddies. I'm feeling antsy because I won't get close to the action today, but it's probably just as well. Seeing him in the cage would only make me want to go a few rounds too. Devon loves fighting. It's obvious to anyone who sees him doing his thing, and that kind of enthusiasm is contagious. Especially for someone like me, who doesn't need any encouragement.

I connect my laptop to the TV and find the right channel. A pair of commentators are discussing the bouts ahead, and I sink onto the sofa to listen. Devon won't be competing for a few hours yet. He's the big event of the night, and there are a dozen or so undercard bouts ahead of him. I tune out the aching of my shoulder and settle in, ready to enjoy myself vicariously through my friend.

By the time I give up on writing for the evening and venture out of my bedroom, Tony is ensconced on the sofa with a collection of healthy snacks on the coffee table and the TV on high volume.

"Who's fighting tonight?" I ask, knowing that someone from the gym is probably competing if he's making the effort to watch it live.

"Devon," he replies, not taking his eyes from the screen as he pats the empty cushion beside him. "You want to join me?"

I think on it for a moment. I've resolved not to get too close to him because it makes it more difficult to ignore our attraction, but I would like to see how Devon goes. "How long before he's on?"

Tony checks his phone. I assume he's looking at the fight card. "Another five fights to go."

"Great. Time to cook." I head to the kitchen, noting I can still see the screen from here. "I'm going to make something quick and easy for dinner. Maybe a burger. Have you eaten?"

"Not yet." He glances over. "Would it be asking too much for you to make me one too?"

"Of course not." I get to work, assembling what we need, and after checking with him, I cook lean chicken for my burger and beef for his. It's nice doing this for him. It feels like I've dropped into the kind of life I've always envisioned for myself, where there's someone to share the mundane parts of my day with. Someone to cook for, and with whom I can debrief after finishing work. I smile at the thought.

Tony and I don't talk while I'm busy in the kitchen. He's engrossed in the event, and I'm listening to the commentators as they dissect each fight. When dinner is ready, I plate both burgers, pass him one, and take the other for myself. I prop it on my lap as I sit beside him.

"Two more before Dev is on," he says, biting into his burger. "This is really fucking good." He speaks around a mouthful of food. I grin, pleased my efforts are being appreciated. "How's the book?"

I grunt because there really aren't any words at this stage. "I'm hoping Devon's fight inspires me."

He raises an eyebrow. "Aren't you writing a historical romance? How is MMA supposed to inspire you?"

I sneak a peek at him. "Because Devon and Harley are couple goals. My couple just isn't meshing, and maybe seeing a real-life example will be what I need to work through it."

He looks at me like I'm nuts. "Let me get this straight. You, the woman who gets all mushy for romance, thinks that the relationship between my teammates is perfect?"

I can hear his disbelief, and I'm not surprised. From the outside, there's nothing obviously romantic about Harley and Devon. They're not cutesy, and they don't always get along, but they're the dream for me because they're real. Harley is a no-nonsense athlete, and Devon is a chronic flirt who doesn't take anything seriously, but together, they work.

"I know it sounds strange, but let me explain." I think about how best to put what's in my head into words. "Dev and Harley are completely in love and committed. They're obsessed with the same sport, and they push each other's buttons in all the right ways. What they have... it suits them." I smile to myself as I remember the last time I saw them together. There was no doubt in my mind they were meant for each other.

"Their relationship isn't what everyone wants," I continue, "including me—but I do want that same depth of feeling. I want someone to care for me the way Harley and Devon care for each other, and to know that I'm the most important thing in the world to that person." My cheeks heat. I've gotten far deeper than I intended. I clear my throat. "Anyway, relationships are about two people who want the same thing and find it together. That's what I need for my fictional couple."

His dark eyes watch me closely. He seems to have forgotten the fight on TV. "You, Luce, are a romantic to the core."

I sigh, wishing that sounded like a compliment. "Guilty as charged. I've tried to turn it off, but I just can't. I love the mushy stuff, and nothing beats a good grand gesture."

He cocks his head, and I feel his gaze as it travels over me like a caress. Suddenly, I feel far too close to him. I cram my burger into my mouth, needing something to focus on.

"What grand gesture would you like someone to make for you?" His question catches me off guard. He winks. "I know you've thought about it. Go on, tell me."

I'm glad it takes a while for me to swallow the mouthful of burger because it gives me time to gather my thoughts. Honestly, I know the answer, but I'm not sure I want to share it. I study him, trying to figure out whether he'll make fun of me. I don't think he will. He might like to tease, but he's a nice guy. Or at least he is when he's not protecting his injury like a bear with a thorn in his paw.

"I've always wanted to be serenaded," I tell him. "But only by a man who can actually sing. That proviso is important. If he can't sing, it's sweet but too cringey."

To my surprise, he doesn't make a flippant comment. Instead, he touches my arm and says softly, "I hope you find what you're looking for."

I catch my breath. His tone says more than his words

ever could. It tells me he's being sincere, but he doubts it will happen.

Most of all, it tells me *he'll* never be the guy who serenades his lady love.

But then, I already know that. So why am I so disappointed?

Chapter Five

TONY

A ringing phone interrupts the set of exercises I'm midway through. I try to recall how many reps I've done. Seven? Eight? It rings again, and I glance over at the screen, spotting Mom's name. Guess I'd better answer.

"Buongiorno," she says in greeting. "How are you, darling? Are you taking care of yourself?"

I grimace. "Everything is fine, Mamma. My shoulder is better than last week, and the beach is nice."

She sighs loudly. "I wish we'd been able to come with you. Such a shame none of us could get leave from work on short notice."

Such a shame, I think wryly.

"I'm managing well. I hope you're not worrying."

She huffs. "Of course I am. It's a mother's prerogative."

"There's no need, I promise."

"You saying that doesn't turn off my maternal instincts," she points out. "It just makes me think you're hiding something."

"Nothing at all." Except an inconvenient attraction to my housemate. "How are things at home?"

"Brilliant!" Her enthusiastic response makes me smile. I'm glad she's happy. "When do you plan to come back?"

"I'm not sure. I won't be able to return to the gym for a couple of months yet."

"But surely you won't stay in Massachusetts until then." She sounds horrified. "All alone, with no family?" Now she's fretting. "And you'll miss my engagement party."

"Your *what?*"

She trills a laugh. "Yes, that's why I called. Kevin and I are having an engagement party in three weeks. Two Saturdays from this one. Please say you'll come. You know how upset I'd be if my only son couldn't make it."

Ah, yes. The guilt card. She plays it well.

I can't refuse without being a bad son. No matter how much I mistrust her whirlwind relationship with good old Kevin, I'll do what I can to support her. She is my mom, after all. Even if she stays true to form and soon ends their fast-paced romance after a series of increasingly intense fights.

"I'll be there, Mamma. I wouldn't miss it."

"*Favolosa!* I have something else to ask you too."

I lie on the floor and stare at the ceiling, the phone to my ear. "What is it?"

"When we have the ceremony, I'd like it if you'd walk me down the aisle, since you're my only beloved son."

Emotion chokes me up. "I'd be honored." Even if I think the marriage is a terrible idea. "I'd love to do that for you."

"*Grazie.* It's going to be wonderful." Excitement thickens her accent. "I've already ordered a dress and started working on a guest list."

I frown. "How big is this wedding going to be?"

"Oh, I don't know. A couple hundred people."

My jaw drops and I sputter.

"I didn't get the big, fairy-tale wedding the first time around," she says. "It was only our closest family, and I've always longed for a do-over. Now's my chance."

"I hope you have the wedding of your dreams." I also hope she hasn't got so carried away in planning it that she's forgotten the realities of married life.

"Thank you, darling." There's a burst of noise in the background, and Mom rattles something off in rapid-fire Italian. While I speak the language, I struggle to follow her when she's going a million miles an hour. My two oldest sisters are more proficient. "Sorry, Antonio, that's Stella. I have to go. Talk later?"

"Of course," I reply dutifully. "Bye, Mamma."

We end the call, and I place the phone on the floor and bury my face in my hands. The situation with Mom is stirring up all kinds of fears and concerns I'd rather keep buried. It's as if she's forgotten the state she was in when Dad left, or the ugly aftermath of Stella, Mia, and Adele's divorces. Stella's husband cheated on her, Mia's emotionally abused her, and Adele's left—understandably—after she slept with his daughter's teacher. None of it had been pretty. All of it had reinforced one irrefutable fact: love doesn't last, and it isn't worth the wreckage.

I get to my feet and ball my fists, wanting badly to throw a few punches at a bag to burn off my frustration. MMA has been my outlet for so long that having it stolen makes me angry. I need to work off excess energy, so I change into a pair of swimming trunks and stride from the bedroom.

"Hey," Lucia says as I emerge onto the deck, where she's once again hunched over her laptop. A furrow forms on her brow. "Is everything okay?" She glances at my shoulder, and I flinch. It seems like this is the story of my life lately. Everyone wants to make sure I'm all right. It's not as if I can explain what's wrong. I'll sound like an asshole if I tell her I don't think my mom should be getting married.

"Nothing a good walk on the beach won't fix," I say.

"Want company?"

I shake my head. "Thanks for the offer, though."

I jog down the stairs at the side of the deck, and instead of heading straight into the water, I walk for ten minutes until I'm confident Lucia won't be able to see me. I don't need her fussing because she thinks I'm overdoing it. I wade into the water until it's deep enough to swim. The first few strokes are painful, but after that, the sensation lessens—perhaps because my muscles loosen up, or perhaps because I become numb to it. Either way, it feels good to be active again.

———

LUCIA

After Tony vanishes down the beach, it's difficult to concentrate. He's clearly upset about something and doesn't want to talk about it, but I can't help feeling like he might need to. Sometimes needs and wants don't align. I try to put him to the back of my mind and focus on my fictional couple, who are deep into an important conversation, but I can't pick up where I left off. I'm too worried.

I reach for my phone and bring up my sister-in-law's number. Tempe knows Tony better than I do. Perhaps she'll be able to shed some light on what's going on.

"Hey, Lucia." She answers just as I'm about to give up. I can hear my niece, Madison, making noises in the background. Madison is a long way from being able to talk, but that doesn't stop her trying. It crosses my mind that Tony could learn a thing or two from the baby in that regard. "Are you enjoying your time at the cottage?"

"Yeah, it's going well."

"And your roommate?" I'd called previously and let her know Tony had turned up. Fortunately, she hadn't made a big deal of it.

"He's why I rang."

"Oh?" She shushes Madison. "Is something wrong?"

"Kind of. I'm not sure." I sigh, wishing there was an easy way for me to voice my concerns that won't sound like I'm making a big deal of nothing. "He's been moody since he arrived. I put it down to the injury at first, but he just had a phone call in his room—I caught a few bits and pieces through the wall—and when it was done, he took off like a demon was on his heels. Do you have any idea what else might be going on?"

"Moody?" Tempe sounds baffled. "Tony? But he's usually so easygoing."

"I know. It's strange, right?"

"Very." Tempe seems as dumbfounded as me. "I have no idea what else could be behind it, sorry. Perhaps it's just the injury. Maybe he got a call from Seth or the doctor with news he didn't want to hear."

"Maybe," I muse. But I think there's more to it than that. I get the impression he's coming to terms with his injury, and this is another beast causing the problem. I could be wrong, though. Other than spending the past week with him, I don't know the guy well. "Thanks anyway. I'll let you get back to Madison."

"I'm glad you called," Tempe says. "Mercy and I miss you. Any idea when you'll be home?"

I scowl. "Whenever the damn book is finished."

She laughs lightly. "You can do it. We have faith in you."

"Thanks, Tempe." Sometimes I think she has no idea what her support means to me. I've never had many friends, and Tempe has quickly become like a sister. "Love you."

She says her goodbyes and hangs up. I push the phone away and look out across the beach. Somewhere, Tony is no doubt doing something stupid to try to work through his emotions in a "tough man" way rather than addressing them properly.

My frustration simmers, and I turn to my computer to hammer out a scene where the hard-headed hero refuses to see the truth that's right in front of him. Meanwhile, the long-suffering heroine encourages him even though she wants to cuff him over the head.

Maybe I'm projecting a little, but I have a feeling many women will relate.

Nearly two hours pass before Tony trudges back up the beach toward the cottage. His complexion is paler than before, and as he draws near, I can see he's gritting his teeth. He doesn't look good.

"Have a nice time?" I ask, not wanting to broach the subject of how unwell he appears in case he's still in a surly mood.

"I overdid it," he mutters. "My shoulder is killing me."

No surprise there. I don't think he knows how to take it easy.

"Are you going to do anything about it?"

He bites his lip, his expression sheepish. "If I call for an emergency appointment, will you take me to the physiotherapist? I don't think I can drive."

My eyes widen. He's asking for help? What happened to the stubborn man I've been living with? I bite my tongue because I'd hate for him to get his guard up when he's only just lowered it enough to be vulnerable with me.

"Absolutely." I'm pretty sure the scene I've been writing will need to be struck from the story anyway. "Just let me know what time you need to be there."

"Thanks." He turns to the cottage entrance, then hesitates and looks back at me. "Sorry for making this your problem. I know I've been stuck in my own head lately, and you shouldn't have to deal with the consequences of that."

I give him a look. "I'd like to think we're friends. Friends help other friends, even when those friends are behaving stupidly." I can't resist adding that last jibe, and he smiles, so I guess he forgives me for it. I shoo him away. "Go call the P.T."

He heads inside, and I pack up my laptop, notebook, and the coffee mug I've been refilling all day. I lock the sliding doors and change into a pair of jeans and a tank top. When I emerge, Tony is waiting in the living room.

"I've booked an appointment for half past two," he says, passing me the keys for the rental car he picked up recently. "We've got ten minutes to get there."

"Perfect. Let's get going."

Chapter Six

TONY

When I leave the physiotherapist's office, Lucia is waiting patiently on a chair outside, reading a book on her phone. She glances up and smiles. There's no hint of strain or irritation in her expression, like many people might have at this point. She hasn't chastised me about how I messed up, even though I can tell she thinks I've acted rashly. Somehow, the fact she hasn't lectured makes me feel worse. Would she be so reserved if I hadn't acted like an ass every time she showed concern?

"All done?" she asks.

"Yeah." I wait for her to get up, so we can walk together. "She said to rest my shoulder for a couple of days and to not overwork it again or I might lose the progress I've made."

"Uh-huh." Lucia sounds dubious about my ability to follow instructions. "And what are you actually going to do?"

"Listen to her," I reply defensively. "I've learned my lesson."

"Good. I'm proud of you for making that decision."

Her words warm my heart. It's strange. I've never craved anyone's approval before, but being thrust into this situation with Lucia, where we're sharing a house and spending most of our time together, seems to have messed with my priorities. "Thanks for being so understanding about the situation. Someone else probably would have told me I was being a jerk and bailed by now."

She stops beside my car and crosses her arms over her chest. "If you think that then you've been spending time with the wrong kind of people. The right kind will stand by you through thick and thin. They don't leave when life gets hard."

That warmth in my heart spreads outward, diffusing through my body. "You're such a sweetheart."

She cocks her head, a blush creeping up her cheeks. "It's just the truth."

I'm not sure it's everyone's truth, but it's her truth, and I love that about her. She's a good person.

I move closer, pinning her to the side of the car, and cup her cheek. "Thank you."

She blinks rapidly. "For what?"

"Being you." I run my thumb across her cheekbone. "Giving me faith in humanity."

She starts to laugh, then stops when she realizes I'm serious. "But—"

"But nothing," I interrupt, knowing she's about to protest that she's not special, which would piss me off because she is. She's incredible, and she doesn't see it. "I know I haven't exactly been a prince, but you've treated me well, and I appreciate that. So just let me share my gratitude, damn it."

Her lips curve into an impish smile, and my chest tightens in response. On impulse, I dip my head and brush my mouth to hers. The kiss is gentle. It draws me in like a bonfire, making me want to get closer. I press against her body, feeling the curve of her breasts against my torso. One of her thighs slips between mine, and a sigh eases from her lips. I drink it up, wanting more.

You shouldn't do this, the voice in my head reminds me. *She deserves better than what you can give her.*

But I can't convince myself to let her go. She tastes as decadent as she looks, and my cock is demanding I claim more. It's not just because she's beautiful, though. Lucia accepts me in a way I'm not used to, and while I know I shouldn't lead her on, I can't help thinking perhaps it isn't coincidence that's brought us together now. With Mom remarrying, I'm at an important juncture of my life. Perhaps Lucia being here, in Provincetown, at the same time as me, is a sign things are going to work out. Maybe Mom's relationship isn't as doomed as I fear. Perhaps Kevin is the right man for her. And if she can move on and have a happily ever after, there might be hope for me too.

Or maybe I'm reading too much into things.

But with Lucia's taste in my mouth and her curves beneath my hands, I allow myself to go with the flow. To stop fighting this thing between us.

Someone toots their car horn, breaking us apart. Lucia trembles beneath my touch and gazes up at me questioningly. I want to reassure her, but I have no idea what we're doing—just that I don't want it to end.

"Let's go home," I suggest.

She gives me a little push, and I realize I'm blocking her in. When I back off, she unlocks the car and gets into the driver seat. I round the hood and sit in the passenger side.

"What was that?" she asks as she starts the engine and pulls out of the parking lot.

"I'm not sure," I say. "I'm sorry if I'm confusing you. I'm confusing me too." I battle to speak my thoughts aloud. "I like you. There's so much about you to admire, and I've been trying not to cross any lines, but I obviously haven't succeeded."

She's focusing on the road, but I can sense her concentration. "Why have you been trying not to cross any lines?"

"Uh." That's not what I expected her to ask. "Because you're a forever girl, and I'm a just-for-now guy. Plus you're Tempe's family, and I wouldn't want things to get messy."

"So you decided for me that I wasn't interested in anything temporary?" Her tone is overly calm, and it makes me hesitate.

"I made the decision not to pursue you," I say carefully. "Because I'm allowed to want someone but decide not to act on it."

She tilts her head. "Fair enough."

"Are you mad?" I ask.

She glances over, visibly surprised. "No. I'm just trying to understand you."

I snort. "Good luck with that. Many have tried, few have succeeded."

"I'm making headway." She reaches across and takes my hand. I'm unprepared for the gesture and find myself twining my fingers between hers before I can think better of it. "Want to talk about whatever happened earlier?"

I give her hand a squeeze and blow out a breath. "Yeah. Maybe that would help."

———

LUCIA

I rein in my natural reaction, which is to celebrate the fact Tony is finally beginning to open up. I don't want to freak him out, so I give him time. The silence drags on. Eventually, I realize he's waiting until we get back to the cottage. When I pull up the drive, he jumps out and heads around to open my door. I stand, finding myself way too close to him, but he just kisses my forehead and backs away, leading me to the cottage entrance with one hand. He unlocks it and we enter and remove our shoes in the hall, then make our way to the living room, where he sits on the sofa and motions for me to join him. When I do, he slings his right arm around my waist and draws me closer. I shut my eyes for a moment, enjoying his touch, and wishing I could rest my head on his chest while I listen to him talk. But that seems too intimate.

"Take your time," I say, wanting him to know there's no rush. This conversation can happen as quickly or as slowly as he likes. I know it will be hard for him. I get the impression he usually avoids difficult topics by flirting or brushing them off so people don't see what's going on in his head. He's like an iceberg. His charming exterior is the only part showing above the water, but beneath is a treasure trove of fears, hopes, and dreams.

He reaches for his water bottle, which he must have left on the coffee table earlier, and takes a drink. He flicks the cap back into place and sets it down again. "There's a reason I'm anti-relationships, and it's not just that I'm a player." He picks at his cuticles as he speaks, not making eye contact. "I honestly don't believe relationships can work long-term."

"What, like *ever*?" I'm stunned—both by his statement and because I didn't expect the conversation to go in this direction. "But there are happy couples all around you. Harley and Dev. Gabe and Sydney. Tempe and Mercy. Leo and Camile."

He shrugs his good shoulder. "None of those relationships have lasted more than a few years."

I frown. "What about Seth and Ashlin?"

Seth and his ex-wife recently remarried.

"It's a cycle. We don't know how long they'll stay together this time."

My mouth opens and closes. I can't believe how cynical he's being. "But surely you don't think that every single relationship is doomed to failure?"

"Kinda, yeah. Or at least, I have until recently."

"Why?"

"My parents." His reply comes too easily, and I flinch. I hadn't been expecting a straight answer. I thought he'd hedge and avoid like he has been since our first day here.

"I'm sorry." I pull away from him so he can see how much I mean it. "What happened with them?"

"They met as backpackers in Germany. She was Italian, he was American. They spent a few months traveling across Europe together. From what I've heard, they were one of those passionate couples who fight and make up over and over again. They thought their behavior was normal. Then Mom got pregnant with Adele and they came to the United States to get married."

"Oh." In my opinion, an accidental pregnancy is never a good thing to base a marriage on. But obviously, as has been the case with Tempe and Mercy, it can work out.

"Yeah. Oh." He shakes his head. "They were off and on for the next couple of decades. When I was twelve, Dad ran off to France with a twenty-two-year-old burlesque dancer. We haven't seen him since."

I absorbed his revelation. It sounded like he'd had a turbulent upbringing, which would make anyone wary. But surely one bad relationship shouldn't sour his entire view of love. "So that made you give up on the idea of a successful marriage?"

He raises a brow as though he can sense my disbelief. "Not completely, but since then, three of my sisters have been married and divorced, and I had to listen to them tear themselves apart over it. One was abused, another had an unfaithful husband, and the oldest was unfaithful herself. It's hard to believe in marriage when you've seen things go wrong so many times."

I nod, because adding those instances to his mother's poor experience, I understand his hesitation. It would be enough to make anyone jaded. But then, hearing his past also makes me hopeful because I know now he isn't fundamentally opposed to the concept of a relationship. He's just scared of being hurt or of hurting someone else. That's an entirely different thing from not wanting to be monogamous. Perhaps we can work through it, if he's willing to try.

"It's reasonable that you're gun-shy after what your family has been through," I say, giving into the temptation to rest my cheek on his chest. His heart thuds steadily beneath my ear.

"Mom is engaged again." His voice rumbles through me.

"She is?" My breathing quickens. Something tells me this is important, which means I need to tread carefully. "How do you feel about it?"

He grunts noncommittally. "I didn't even meet Kevin before he popped the question." He pauses, then adds, "They told me the night of my last fight."

"Shit." That was the fight where he'd been injured. I wonder if having the news dropped on him played a role in his performance in the cage. Fighters need to be completely in the zone, and his thoughts must have been all over the place. I hesitate, deciding not to ask. If he wants to bring it up, he will. "Would you feel better about the engagement if you knew more about Kevin?"

He pulls a face, as though the idea of getting to know his mother's fiancée pains him. "Maybe a bit. Honestly, I don't know that I'd ever feel good about it, but the way they're diving into things so quickly makes me worry she's going to have regrets." He huffs. "This is what she does.

She gets carried away and glosses over any indication that something isn't going to work. Then, when she can't ignore the problems anymore, she loses her temper. There are fights. Then she moves on." He holds my gaze. "Every. Single. Time. Although, to be fair, this is the first time since my dad that she's got engaged."

"Oh. I can see why you're worried." Given what he's told me, it makes sense he'd be concerned about the speed of things and need time to get used to having someone around before they officially became part of the family. But on the other hand, his parents must have been together for a long time, and they still ended badly, so surely he can see that longevity of a relationship doesn't necessarily mean it won't go wrong. "What else would make you more comfortable with him?"

"I don't know." He sounds weary, and I hate it. I want to bundle him up and protect him from everything. Unfortunately, this engagement is going ahead whether or not he's on board, so he can't avoid it, and I won't coddle him. "Perhaps if he'd made an effort to introduce himself before he gave her a ring."

"Unfortunately, we can't go back in time and ask him to do that, so as things are, what would make you less apprehensive?"

He growls in frustration. "I don't know." The words are terse, but they're aimed at himself rather than me. "Maybe if I understood why they're moving so fast. I know Mom is naturally impulsive, but I don't see why they're in a rush. Two weeks ago I didn't know he existed, and now they're planning an engagement party? I've got whiplash."

I wriggle closer to him, offering what comfort I can, and enjoy the way his arm firms around my waist. "Have you thought about talking to your mom? I'm sure she'd be open to discussing it with you."

I expect him to dismiss the suggestion, but to my

surprise, he seems to consider it. "Maybe. I haven't said anything yet because I didn't want to upset her, but I think she'd be more upset if she knew I was secretly stressing out."

"Exactly." I smile. "Give it a try and see how it goes. She loves you, and your approval probably means something to her."

He kisses my forehead, and butterflies cluster in my stomach. There's a new ease between us and a sense of intimacy we haven't previously had, but we haven't discussed what it means. I'm trying not to worry. All I need to know for certain is Tony sees me—really sees me—and appreciates the way I am. Anything else can come later.

Chapter Seven

When I wake the following morning—from a surprisingly good sleep despite the pain in my shoulder—I'm more emotionally balanced than yesterday. I dress in sweatpants and a T-shirt and open the curtains in the main bedroom. The view of the beach is stunning, with a few glimmers of gold on the water and pink streaks in the sky above it. I soak in the serenity for a few moments, listening to the gurgle of waves on the sand and watching the seabirds soar on a light breeze.

Last night, I decided I'd call Mom today. I'd expected to feel more nervous about it, but find I'm at peace with my choice. I sit on the edge of the bed, tap Mom's number on my cell phone, and wait for the call to connect.

"Tony!" she exclaims. "You've caught me just before work."

Oops. I'd forgotten about work and the time zone difference between us. I guess I've started to take the relaxed pace of beach life for granted. "Do you have a minute for a quick chat?"

She scoffs. "I always have time for my children."

"Thanks." For all that she's a hurricane of a woman, she is a loving and devoted mother. "I just want to say that I'm happy for you, and I'd like to hear more about Kevin. I want to get to know him if he's going to be an important part of your life."

"*Our* lives," she corrects. "But yes, I understand your meaning. If you suddenly had a fiancée, I'd be curious about her." She makes a sound of displeasure. "But darling, you were the one who took yourself off to Massachusetts. If you'd stayed here, Kevin and I could have visited every night to check on you, and you'd have had plenty of opportunity to get to know him better."

She has a point. But perhaps part of the reason I was so eager to leave is I didn't want to spend more time with Kevin. I'd hoped if I buried my head in the sand, he might vanish. But clearly that wasn't the right approach.

"I know. But will you tell me more about him anyway?"

"Yes." She's unusually quiet for a moment, gathering her thoughts. "He's an accountant. I met him during a business meeting at Moretti's." Moretti's is the Italian diner where Mom works as a cook. "He has two sons around your age. He's lovely, Tony." She sighs happily, and I feel bad for being a cynic. "He opens doors for me and listens to what I have to say. He's a gentleman. I didn't think I'd ever find one of those, but somehow I have. He likes to cook too. We've been teaching each other recipes. And he has a gorgeous dog."

I grin at the thought of Mom with a dog. She's never been the type for pets. But then my smile fades. What if the dog becomes a bone of contention for them? You never know what might cause problems. Overlooking a potential issue when it arises is another pattern of hers.

"I assume he's divorced," I say, getting back on track. Something obviously wasn't right with perfect Kevin, or he'd still be with his ex.

"He's a widower." Mom's voice is soft and a little sad. "He loved his late wife very much. She died of cancer five years ago."

"That must have been awful." Once again, I feel like a jerk for making assumptions.

"Yes." She draws in a shuddering breath. "We've talked about it a lot. He has photos of her around the house."

"And that doesn't bother you?"

"Why would it?" She honestly sounds confused. "She was an important part of his life, and he loved her with all his heart. I would never interfere with him remembering her the way she deserves to be. The fact he loved her doesn't mean he can't love me too." Her tone turns chiding. "The human heart has an infinite capacity for love. He can love both of us, the same way I have enough love for you and your sisters. There is no limit."

"Love you, Mamma." This conversation hasn't gone the way I intended, but I can't bring myself to regret it. She's said things I needed to hear. "We should get together for a meal when I'm back in the city."

"I'd like that." There's warmth in her voice, and I'm glad I've made an effort to reach out.

"Goodbye. Have a nice day."

"Ciao." She ends the call.

I slip the phone into my pocket and head to the living area. Lucia is sitting on the sofa, her laptop on her knees, totally engrossed. I walk past her to the kitchen, and she doesn't seem to notice. For once, the story seems to be coming easily to her, and I don't want to interrupt, so I leave her to it and prepare a batch of coffee. While the coffee is brewing, I search the cupboards for a waffle iron, pleased when I find one. I mix together ingredients for basic waffles and locate maple syrup in the pantry and bacon in the refrigerator. I add a few strips of bacon to a frying pan and serve two mugs of coffee. Then, when the waffle iron is hot, I pour batter in and wait for it to cook.

I lean against the kitchen counter and watch Lucia work. After a few minutes, her nose starts to twitch. The tapping of her fingers on the keyboard slows. She glances over and her eyes light up at the sight of coffee.

"That smells amazing!" She types a few more words, then puts her laptop on the coffee table and joins me. I push one of the mugs toward her, and she inhales deeply. "You know the way to a girl's heart, Tony Romano."

A zing of gratification shoots through me. I shouldn't take her comment too seriously. It was a throwaway remark. But damn if I don't want to know the path to Lucia's heart. She turns me inside out like no one else I've met, and I want more of her.

Placing a hand on her hip, I guide her closer for a kiss. The taste of coffee is fresh on her lips, but there's an underlying sweetness that's all her. She sets the coffee aside and steps closer, pulling me down for a proper kiss. The type with tongues and panted breaths and soft moans.

The waffle iron pings.

We break apart, both breathing heavily. She wets her lips, and the glimpse of her pink tongue makes me hard. There's no hiding her effect on me when I'm wearing such loose pants, but she doesn't point it out. Instead, she stretches on her toes and drops one last kiss on my cheek, then goes to the waffle iron. I step up behind her, resting my hands on her hips, and nuzzle the back of her neck.

"Stop it." She laughs. "I'm hungry, and I'll never get breakfast if you keep that up."

"Doesn't sound so bad to me," I murmur, but I ease back and let her plate up the waffles and bacon, drizzling plenty of maple syrup over the one I assume she's decided is hers.

She passes me the other plate and we make our way to

the deck by silent agreement. We eat waffles to the sound-track of waves.

"It looks like you're finally making some progress," I say.

She smiles. "The story is starting to fall into place."

"That's great." Although I have a pinch of dread at the reminder that when she finishes, she'll have no reason to stay here. Selfishly, I don't want her to leave. "Maybe we can head into town together later," I suggest, wanting to make the most of whatever time I have with her.

"That sounds nice."

"Then it's a date." I stiffen at my turn of phrase, but then I realize I really want our outing to be a date. Maybe my thoughts about fate bringing us together weren't too far off. This feels really good, and I don't want it to end.

***

LUCIA

A few hours later, I run out of steam for the day and set my writing aside. I've been worried Tony might grow impatient, but when I raised it with him, he said he didn't care how much time I needed to spend writing before I'd be ready to leave.

When I return inside from the deck, he's sprawled on the living room floor, reading a brochure about the local area.

"Scoping out stuff for us to do?" I ask, hovering over him.

He nods. "I've found a couple of things that look good. Are you done for the day?"

"For now, anyway." I might pick back up later, but writing expends a lot of creative energy, and it's time to refill the well.

"Great." He clambers awkwardly to his feet, managing

not to put any weight on his shoulder. "I'll just grab a jacket. You might want to do the same for one of the activities I have in mind."

"Ooh, intriguing. What is it?"

He winks. "I'll tell you later. Don't want to spoil the surprise."

I head to the bedroom and, not knowing what he has planned, choose a lightweight jacket from my suitcase—it's still summer, after all—then swap my dress for shorts and a top. I check that my purse and phone are in my handbag and take it back to the living room. Tony is waiting on the sofa. He has a jacket tucked under one arm and stands as I approach.

"Would you rather walk or drive?" I ask.

"Walk," he replies. "It's a beautiful day for it."

I tilt my head to smile up at him. "I hoped you'd say that."

He gestures for me to precede him down the hall. I open the front door, and he locks it behind us. Then, to my surprise, he reaches down and takes my hand in his. I jolt at the unexpected contact, but when he doesn't release me, I allow myself to enjoy it. His palm is hot against mine and much larger. It's strong and capable, just like the rest of him.

And yes, it's sexy too.

As we walk, he tells me about his conversation with his mother. I'm glad he followed through on it. I'd been concerned he might have changed his mind today, but it sounds like he's feeling more at ease with the situation, even if he isn't entirely comfortable with it. When he finishes recounting the call, I ask him questions about his mom and sisters. I can't imagine growing up in such a large household. Even before my parents died, our family was on the quieter side. I always had my nose in a book, and Mercy spent his high school years studying his ass off to get into college. By contrast, the Romano family sounds loud and colorful and hilarious. I love listening to stories about the trouble they got into—especially him and his youngest sister, Bianca. It seems they have a lot in common, including a mistrust of relationships, although I'm hoping Tony's hesitation in that area will lessen.

I like him. I know I shouldn't get too attached because he's made it clear he isn't anyone's Mr. Happily Ever After, but my heart doesn't seem to care what he says. It just wants him. And maybe that's not the worst thing. I could enjoy Mr. Right Now, and there's always a chance it could turn into more, but I won't count on that.

We stop at a gelato shop and each get a cone. He opts for citrus while I select old-fashioned hazelnut chocolate, then we stroll along Commercial Street together, eating and talking. When I finish my gelato, I lick my fingers clean.

Tony digs in his pocket and passes me a napkin. "Here."

"Thanks." My cheeks heat. "I always make a mess with ice cream."

He shrugs his uninjured shoulder. "Part of the joy of eating it, in my opinion."

My heart expands. Even his ice cream philosophy meshes with mine.

Not that I should read into it.

Sighing, I remind myself this is a holiday romance—at most.

"That's an awfully big sigh for someone who's about to go on a cruise around the coastline," Tony says.

My eyes shoot to his. "What?"

He nods toward the building on the opposite side of the street. There's a poster showing a group of people on a motorboat in the window. "Surprise."

I stare at it, then back at him. "Wait, seriously?"

"Yeah." He grabs my hand and tugs me across the street toward it. "Come on. We're booked for the ride that's departing soon."

"But… what? How?"

"I called and booked it while you were changing clothes." He grins. "I knew approximately how long it would take us to get here."

I gape at him. "You sneak!"

"But you like it."

"I do," I agree. "This is really sweet. Thank you."

His smile softens and he clasps my hand a bit tighter. "I think we could both use some fun."

He leads me into the building and sorts out details with the woman at the desk while I peruse photographs layered several deep on a pin-board. They show smiling people with the ocean behind them. I reach for a photo of a couple about to kiss and trace the outline of their faces with my fingertip. They're so absorbed in each other it's like the camera doesn't exist.

That's what I want.

"Luce," Tony calls. "Come over here. We need to get fitted with life jackets."

Tearing my gaze from the couple, I join him. The next ten minutes are a blur as we sort out our gear, introduce ourselves to the other people on our trip, and load into a van to head down to the water. It's only once we're about to board the boat that I feel like I can breathe properly again. I take Tony's hand as he helps me on. It's larger than I'd thought, based on the photos, but still small enough that I'll be able to see everybody at all times. The seats are in rows, with a bench around the edge, facing the water. Tony and I sit on the bench. I haven't been on a boat before, and my stomach rolls as it moves on the waves. Tony seems more comfortable than me. I know his family has made a couple of trips to Italy to visit relatives who live near lakes, so perhaps he's been out on the water before.

"You're sure we'll be safe here?" I ask, gesturing to our position.

He kisses the tip of my nose. "We'll be fine."

The boat's skipper speaks through a microphone system, getting our attention. He welcomes us and does a brief talk about safety, which eases my nerves and helps the excitement shine through. Soon after, the engine hums to life, and we slowly move forward. I grip the edge of the seat tightly to steady myself. Tony rests a hand on my thigh, and when I meet his eyes, I can see the reassurance there. He won't let me go overboard.

The boat picks up speed, and we pass the harbor and marina. I keep my gaze trained on the coast, where the larger commercial and industrial buildings eventually give way to smaller private homes and lodges. People stroll along the sand and swim in the shallows. We bounce on the crests of waves as the skipper takes us further out. Gaining confidence, I lean over the edge to watch the churning white water along the side of the vessel, then look up at Tony and beam. My heart is racing, and I love the sensation of the wind in my face—although I do wish I'd brought sunglasses.

"Having fun?" he asks with a matching grin.

"This is awesome." The views are growing more rural, and I catch sight of a tall white building near the landward edge of the sand. "Hey, look at that."

He turns and raises a hand to shield his eyes. "That's the Provincetown lighthouse."

As we draw closer, I can see it's rectangular with a circular addition on top—presumably either where the light comes from or where a person is supposed to man the machinery. It's rustic. Beautiful, in a strange way. Like a reminder of another time.

Tony squeezes my knee. "Want a photo?"

"Yes, please." I pass him my phone and sit still while he positions himself so he can fit both me and the lighthouse into the picture. "Would you like one too?" I ask when he's done.

"Only if you're in it with me."

"Okay." My insides flutter in a way that has nothing to do with the boat or the scenery. He wants a photo with me?

He hands me my phone and holds his own out in front of us, lining up a shot. He snaps it and shows me. "What do you think?"

My heart gives a thump at how good we look together, but then something twists in my gut when I realize how obvious the adoration in my expression is. Even though I'm looking at the camera, my smile is soft, and I'm leaning toward him as though he's the center of my world.

Uh-oh.

I hope Tony can't see the same thing, because it's scary. Nothing about my body language says casual.

"It's nice," I choke out, realizing he's waiting for an answer.

He frowns like he can sense my discomfort, but he doesn't push me to elaborate. Instead, he tucks the phone back into his pocket and slings his uninjured arm around my shoulders. My body melts into his automatically, and the nerves in my stomach multiply.

I'm in trouble.

Chapter Eight

When the boat returns to the jetty we departed from, we all climb off and get back into the van bound for the tour company's office. Lucia is quiet, and when I ask, she says she's tired. I am too, so I organize a ride from the office back to the cottage while we're in transit. I've had a great day with her, and I'm hoping she feels the same. For the first time in my adult life, I'm feeling optimistic about a future with someone. I want to see more of her.

When she's finished her book and my shoulder has healed, I don't want us to go back to being polite acquaintances. I don't know if she's on the same page, though. I get the sense she's holding back. Something happened on the boat, and she's been on edge ever since. I thought I was imagining it at first, but when I offer her a hand to help her out of the van, and she jumps in surprise, I know I'm not.

Our ride is already parked nearby, so we hurry over to it and slide into the back seat. The driver, a man around our age, glances back to say hi. His eyes widen as they land on Lucia.

"Hey there." He waits for her to look at him before continuing. "Where can I take you today?" He should already have the address from the app, but Lucia rattles it off anyway. I narrow my eyes as he turns and starts the car. "What have you guys been up to this afternoon?"

"We went out on a cruise around the coast," I reply.

"Nice." He steals a look at Lucia in the rearview mirror. "How'd you enjoy that, sweetheart?"

Her eyebrows knit together, and I hope she's as put off by the endearment as I am. "It was lovely. My first time on a motorboat, but it definitely won't be my last."

"The ocean around here is pretty spectacular," he says. "Have you been in town for long?"

"About a week and a half," I say at the same time as Lucia chimes in with, "A little under a month."

He looks over his shoulder, obviously curious at the discrepancy. A little *too* curious, in my opinion. "So you're not staying together?"

"We are." I correct him, because damned if I'm going to let this asshole try to put the moves on Lucia right under my nose. "We just arrived at different times."

"Huh."

The way he says it makes me wish I'd sat on the other side of the car, so I could wrap my arm around her. As it is, I have to settle for resting my palm on her thigh and stroking the silken skin at the hem of her shorts. She gives me a weird look, probably wondering what I'm up to.

"What brings you to Provincetown?" the driver asks.

Lucia starts to answer, and the edges of my mouth tense, knowing whatever she says will no doubt make it clear we aren't together. She hesitates, watching me with interest, and then surprises me. "It's a working holiday. I'm finishing up a project while Tony takes time out to recover from an injury. He's a professional MMA fighter."

"Ah." The guy is beginning to sound nervous. He glances back again and does a double take. "Wait. Are you Antonio Romano?"

"Yeah, that's me."

"Oh, man." A bead of sweat rolls down the side of his forehead. "I heard you'd been injured. You look fine."

"I'm doing well." I don't give him any more information, but when he catches my eyes in the mirror, I glare. Fortunately, we're nearing the cottage.

He clears his throat. "Yes, well, I hope you two enjoy the rest of your holiday." He pulls to the side of the road, suddenly eager for us to disembark. I get out and reach back for Lucia. Her eyes twinkle as she lets me guide her from the car. The door is barely shut before he takes off.

"You're ridiculous," she tells me as he screeches away. "There was no need for that."

"Agree to disagree."

She pins me with a look. "I'm not going to run off with a random man." She breaks into a smile. "But it's flattering that you got a tiny bit jealous."

I pout. *Jealous?* I'm not the guy who gets jealous. I'm the one who moves easily from one conquest to another and leaves them smiling behind me. But when it comes to Lucia, I can't stomach the thought of moving on the way I used to. I'm confident she isn't the kind of person who has casual affairs, so whatever is happening between us means something to her. Meanwhile, I feel a bit guilty because I have a history of skipping from one bed to another. For once, I wish I hadn't been so promiscuous because it gives her reason to doubt where my mind is at. As far as she knows, this could all be another fling to me, and she needs to be aware this is different.

I take her hand. "I did get jealous," I confess. "But only because you matter. This isn't some vacation romance. I'm not sure what it is yet, because I haven't done anything like it before, but I care for you." I swallow. "I want you."

Her smile is breathtaking. "I want you too," she says, and then she kisses me, and all rational thought goes out the window.

I start to lift her but think better of it. Instead, I lead her to the front door. When her back hits it, she grabs my face between her palms. My tongue plunges into her mouth, staking a claim I don't have any right to make. She squirms in my arms, trying to get closer. My dick is an iron rod, aching to break through the layers of fabric between us. Lucia makes soft sounds of lust in my ear, driving me crazy.

"Wait a sec." I search my pockets for the key and open the door. She grabs my hand and tugs me to the spare bedroom. The place smells of her, and it sets my senses alight. I lie on the bed, on my good side, ignoring a slight twinge in my shoulder. Lucia pulls her top off before lying opposite me.

My mouth waters. Her body is a curvy little gift, and I want to unwrap it. She has full hips, and her tits are more than a handful. The bra hardly contains them. I stroke a hand along her side, and she shivers, her vivid eyes darkening with desire. I nuzzle the crook of her neck, inhaling her scent, and rub my lips over the satiny skin. She shudders and a sigh escapes her. My cock jerks in excitement. She responds so sweetly to every touch.

I graze my teeth over the cord of her neck and pepper kisses up her throat until I reach her lips. She takes my mouth hungrily, her hands disappearing beneath the hem of my T-shirt and smoothing up my abdomen. My muscles clench and release as she drags her fingernails over the ridges of my abs.

"You're so sexy," she whispers. "I want to lick you all over."

I palm my dick and try to calm my ragged breathing. "Do it," I urge.

Hesitantly, she grabs my shirt and draws it up. When she gets to my chest, she stops and lets me wrestle out of it. Her pupils dilate as she stares at my torso, then her eyes journey back to mine. "Beautiful."

My lips twitch. "I think that's what I'm supposed to say."

She doesn't seem to care who's saying what. She wriggles down the bed and licks along the grooves of my muscles. I release a shaky breath. Her tongue dips into the V that points to my groin, and she traces it to my waistband, dropping kisses along the edge. Tormenting me.

"Please, Luce," I beg. "I need your mouth."

I feel her smile against my stomach. "You have it."

I growl in frustration. "I want it on my cock."

"Demanding," she tsks, but she slowly undoes the fly of my jeans and starts to ease them down. I help her get them off and begin to reach for my underwear, but she mouths my erection through the fabric, and I gasp. The head of my cock is visible beneath the elastic. It leaks precum as she flicks her tongue against the tip.

"*Fuck*," I hiss, my hips instinctively rocking. She pulls my underwear down, and I kick them off. She licks a stripe along the length of the shaft and closes her eyes as though she's savoring the taste. I'm torn between wanting to shove into her mouth versus shifting her around so I can sample her the same way she is me. But then she takes me deeper, and I can't think of anything except the hot, wet suction pulsing around me. My hands bury in her hair.

"Fuck, that's good," I encourage her with muttered praise. "Just like that, baby. *Damn*."

I pull her off when she swallows me a little too well and pressure starts to build at the base of my spine. Her lips curl with feminine pride, and when she licks them, it's all I can do not to come.

"Sit on my face," I order.

She blinks, startled. "What?"

"Please, baby. I need to taste you, and I can't put any weight on my arm at the moment."

"Um, okay." A blush is spreading from her cheeks down her neck, but she straddles me and positions her slick pussy over my face despite her obvious hesitation. I take a moment to get a hold of myself. She's trusting me, and I need to make this good for her.

I use my tongue on her, and she writhes, her hips stuttering with each swipe. I open my mouth and let her ride it, lavishing open-mouthed kisses on her while she bucks and whimpers. When she draws tight and I sense she's near to coming, I ease her off me. Her expression is wild, her eyes dark and glazed.

"Do you have protection?" I ask, since we're in her room.

The question takes a moment to penetrate her lust-drunk state, but then she nods and gets off me, collecting her purse from the bag on the floor and producing a condom from it.

"Like that," she says, directing me onto my back. She tears the condom packet open, tosses the foil aside, and rolls the rubber down my length. "I'll be on top." She winks. "It's my favorite."

I must have won the fucking lottery. I know she's conscious of my sore shoulder, but as she positions herself over me and lowers onto my cock, the sharp breaths falling from her lips make it clear she loves the way I fill her. When I'm all the way inside, she pauses for a moment, her eyes closed.

"God, you feel so good." She raises up and glides down again. I rocket up into a sitting position, the tight clasp of her body almost too much to bear. I draw her closer with my strong arm, using my other hand to roll one of her nipples between my thumb and forefinger. She cries out, her eyes locking on mine. They're so hot. As she holds my gaze, her hips work frantically, riding my cock, and I know I won't be able to hold out for much longer.

"Lucia," I whisper, tasting her lips again. I suck the lower one and run my tongue along it. "You're incredible. You make me feel so much."

Emotion gleams in her stunning eyes, but she seems to be beyond words. Unerringly, I find her clit and massage it in gentle circles. Her head drops back, and it's only my arm around her waist that keeps her in place. Her channel tightens, clamping and releasing as she comes. The tight clasp sends me over the edge, and I bury my face in the side of her neck as I spurt inside her.

She collapses forward, resting her head against me. We stay that way for several moments, holding each other while we catch our breath. When I start to soften inside her, she climbs off my lap and flops onto the bed. Reluctantly, I leave her for long enough to dispose of the condom in the bathroom, and then I return and lie alongside her, wrapping myself around her body. Neither of us speaks. I think we're both processing what happened and the fact that everything between us has irrevocably changed. There's no going back now, and I, for one, am glad of that.

Lucia

Tony and I pass the rest of the day in bed. We spend hours learning each other's bodies, then fall into a sated sleep. In the morning, I wake feeling well-used but wonderful. As I roll over to take in Tony's face in the dim light of dawn, nerves shoot through me unexpectedly.

I'm falling for him.

He said yesterday that I matter and this isn't just casual, but he's never had a relationship before, so it's unchartered territory. What if his fear of hurting someone or being hurt comes back in full force and he's not able to put it aside and see where this thing goes?

His eyelids flutter open, and dark eyes meet mine. The warmth and affection in them make me feel silly for worrying, even if I know it's justified.

"Did you sleep well?" he asks.

"Better than I have in ages," I admit. "You must have worn me out."

He gives a self-satisfied smile. "Damn right, I did." He curves a hand around my face and kisses me sweetly. "Good morning."

"This is the best morning," I say. "Not just a good morning."

His smile widens. "Agreed."

I cuddle close to him and breathe in sleepy man and the faint musk of sex.

"I've been thinking," he begins. I stiffen, immediately on alert. Is this the part where he backtracks from what he said yesterday? "I'd really like it if you'd come to Mom's engagement party as my date."

My tension dissipates. "Seriously? You want that?"

"Well, yeah." He raises himself up on his good shoulder. "I want to keep seeing you, and maybe it's too fast, I don't know what's normal, but I'd like you to meet my family. Plus, having your support would mean a lot." His expression turns wry. "The party might not be easy for me."

"Then absolutely, I'll be there." I stretch up to kiss him.

It's supposed to be chaste, but he deepens the caress, and any thought of backing off vanishes from my mind.

"Thank you," he murmurs.

"You're very welcome."

Finally, I allow hope to infiltrate my heart. I've been wary of believing in this daydream-worthy romance we seem to have fallen into, but against all odds, Tony Romano might be my forever man.

Chapter Nine

LUCIA

After Tony and I spent our first night together, the book absolutely pours out of me. It seems like all I needed to give new life to my fictional romance was a real-world romance of my own. For three weeks, I write all morning, explore Provincetown with Tony in the afternoon, and make love at night. His shoulder is steadily improving with the help of the physiotherapist, and he's in good shape to return to the gym in another month or so. They doubt he'll need to be referred for surgery, although that will need to be confirmed by his usual physiotherapist back in Las Vegas.

Now, it's Thursday, and I've been feeling oddly melancholy since I typed The End a couple of hours ago. The timing worked out well because we have a flight home scheduled for tomorrow morning, and it's his mother's engagement party on Saturday. But I've enjoyed myself more in the past several weeks than I have in a long time, and it feels like our period of easy happiness is drawing to a close. When we're back in Las Vegas, I won't wake and see Tony's face first thing in the morning. I won't fall asleep in his arms every night. I'll be at my place, and he'll be at his. Perhaps some nights we'll stay together, but we haven't discussed what that might look like, and I know for certain it won't be the idyllic existence we've been living, which has been like something out of one of my deepest fantasies.

Unfortunately, we haven't discussed what our relationship will look like, full stop. All I know is we want to continue to see each other, and I'll be at the party on Saturday. Beyond that, I have some important questions. Like, are we exclusive? How often will we see each other? When will we tell our mutual friends we're dating? We've kept it on the down low so far. Me, out of caution, and him, presumably out of habit.

I lift my suitcase onto the bed and fold laundry into it, leaving out a set of clothes to wear tomorrow. I've already packed my laptop and electronics. I want to be as ready as possible so I can relax with Tony tonight and not have to worry about doing much before we leave for the airport. I add the toiletries I won't need and leave the suitcase on the bed. I'm hoping to spend tonight in the master suite with Tony, so it shouldn't matter if I use the bed for storage.

Gathering my courage, I make my way through the living area and into the main bedroom. Tony is standing in front of the window, stretching his shoulder. He glances over and smiles when he sees me. "Hey, gorgeous. Done packing?"

"For the most part." I bite my lip, knowing I need to speak up about the things that have been weighing on my mind but not quite sure how to start.

He crosses the room and kisses my cheek. "What's going on? You seem nervous."

"I am, a bit," I confess. I take his hand and lead him to the bed. I sit on the edge, and he joins me. I steel myself. This is going to be fine. I care about Tony, and he cares about me. I'm not going to force him into anything, but I think I deserve a relationship, and I want one long-term. I need to know if he sees us ending up there eventually.

"Is everything okay?" he asks, his brow furrowed.

"Yes." My throat is dry, so I swallow. "When we get back to Vegas, what do you want our relationship to look like?" The grooves in his forehead deepen, but I forge ahead. "Are we dating? If so, are we open to dating other people? Will we see each other every day? Every week? What do you want to tell our families?"

He studies me intently, but he hasn't run for the exit, which is a good start. "Is this what's been bothering you?"

"Maybe." My voice is small. I'm hesitant about coming on too strong, but I need to know what to expect from him.

"Baby." He sounds exasperated. "You could have asked me sooner." He raises my hand to his mouth and kisses the back of it.

"I didn't want to pressure you."

He winces. "Okay, I get where you're coming from, but I'm sorry I made you feel like you couldn't ask. I'm not going to make any promises because I'm new at this, but I'm falling for you, Luce, and I want to see where it goes." His jaw tightens. "We'd better be exclusive, or I'll break my promise not to go back to fighting too soon, because I couldn't stand to see you with anyone else."

"Good." My insides dance happily at his words. He's falling for me. Just like I am for him. That reassures me more than anything. "Because I don't want you to be with any other women either."

"I won't be," he promises. "For as long as I'm with you, it's just us."

For as long as I'm with you.

The flutters in my stomach die off. I know he means the promise in a positive way, but all I can hear is the possibility of us ending. I try not to dwell on it. Once he sees how well we fit into each other's lives, he won't be able to imagine going our separate ways. I just have to trust in that.

———

Tony

I rest against the doorframe, watching Lucia prepare for Mom's engagement party. Her hair is loose around her shoulders, and she looks beautiful in a pale purple dress. I can't tear my gaze from her. She applies pink lipstick and rubs her lips together, then blows a kiss at me in the mirror. My eyes lock on hers, which look even more vividly blue than usual thanks to eyeliner, and the heat in the bedroom ratchets up. I wish we didn't have to put in an appearance tonight. I'd much rather take her somewhere private where we could dance until we can't stand the tension and then fuck like bunnies for the rest of the night. Unfortunately, I spoke to Mom earlier, so she's expecting both of us to be present.

"You're sure this is okay?" Lucia asks, looking down at herself.

"You're perfect, sweetheart." Smooth legs, shapely thighs, and an intriguing shadow between her breasts. But the tightness around her eyes and mouth tells me she's still worried. I go to her and put my hands on her waist. "What's on your mind?"

She sighs. "It's nothing. Just… events like this are hard for me sometimes. I don't have much practice around big families, so I'm not sure what to expect, and then there's the fact they remind me I'm never going to be able to do this sort of thing with my own mom and dad."

"Oh, honey." I pull her into my arms and hold her. "I didn't even think of that." Of course being around a big, crazy family to celebrate a major milestone would be hard for her. "Are you sure you want to go?"

She nods. "Yes. I just want you to know where my head is at. If I get a bit quiet, it's not because of anything you've said or done."

"Okay." I kiss her forehead. "I'll keep that in mind. As for them liking you, they're going to adore you. Mom will want to adopt you, and my sisters will get you in their clutches and never let you go."

Her lips tilt up, and I consider that a success. "I'm looking forward to meeting them."

"You say that now. They can be pretty overwhelming."

"Maybe that's what I need." She pulls away from me and tucks the lipstick into her clutch. "I'm ready to go."

"We can take a few moments to recalibrate if you need." I don't want to rush her. Especially if she's feeling fragile.

"Nope, I'm ready to do this." She lifts her chin. "Come on, tough guy."

"All right, then." I grab our jackets from where they're hanging on the back of the door, and we head down the front stairs to the street, where my car is parked. I open the passenger door for her and then get into the driver's side.

It takes a while to drive to the venue—they've chosen to hold the party at one of the hotels downtown—but we find a parking spot without too much trouble and enter together. I glance at my phone, skimming the instructions Mom sent for how to find the conference room where the party is being held. She asked for my sisters and me to be here early to help with any last-minute setup and to welcome the guests. We take the elevator up a couple of stories, and we're heading down a corridor when we hear raised voices.

The hairs on the back of my neck prickle as I recognize Mom's as one of them. I break into a jog and hurry around the corner. At the end of the corridor are a set of double doors. The noise is coming from behind them. I barge in, coming to an abrupt halt at the sight of Mom and Kevin facing off against each other. Mia and Bianca are plastered to the wall, trying to disappear into the background, and one of the hotel's staff members is hovering awkwardly nearby.

Oh shit. I knew this was going to happen. I just fucking knew it.

"I don't know where the damn cake is!" Kevin shouts. He's red in the face and sweating.

I take a step forward, wanting to deck him for talking to Mom that way, but Lucia arrives beside me, panting, and grabs my elbow.

"What's going on?" she asks.

"I don't know," I murmur as Mom marches toward Kevin and lets loose a stream of angry Italian.

"Oh, wow." Lucia's eyes widen. "She's *not* happy."

"You should know where the cake is," Mom cries in English. "It was your job to pick it up."

"Just like it was supposedly my job to let the caterers know about any special dietary requirements, and to organize accommodation for everyone coming from out of town, and to send the guest list to the hotel?" he demands, looking like there's a very real risk of him stroking out.

"Yes!" Mom exclaims. "It's not too much to ask for you to do your part to make sure today is perfect."

He pivots and storms away, with her following close behind. "Does it really matter if a couple of things don't get done? It's only the engagement party."

"*Only* the engagement party?"

Kevin seems to realize he's put his foot in his mouth. He stops walking and holds his hands up defensively. "Wait a second. Gia, you know that's not what I meant."

"Isn't it?" she challenges, all five and a half feet of her getting up in his face. "It's our wedding. I want everything to be perfect, including the engagement party, and I shouldn't have to do it all myself."

Kevin reaches for her, but she shoots invisible lasers from her eyes, and he drops his hands. "I didn't even want a big wedding," he protests, shoving his foot even further into his mouth. "You're the one who asked for an engagement party. I'd be happy to marry you in front of an Elvis impersonator in one of those drive-through chapels."

"You didn't want this?" Mom looks crestfallen, and my stomach bottoms out. Any remaining optimism I'd been carefully cultivating for the past few weeks goes up in smoke. Everything is falling apart, just like I predicted. This should be one of the happiest moments of their lives, yet they're yelling at each other instead of cherishing it because they rushed into something without taking the time to talk it through and get to know each other better.

It's ridiculous how disappointed I am. I expected this. I've been waiting for it to happen since they announced the engagement, but secretly, I wanted them to be successful, because if Mom could find someone to spend her life with, then maybe I could too. Instead, they're reinforcing what I've forever known to be true.

People hurt each other. Always.

"Maybe we should cancel the party." Mom has deflated. She's not being overdramatic. She might seriously call everything off even though the guests are due to start arriving in ten minutes.

"Gia—"

I don't hear the rest of what Kevin says because Lucia grabs my hand and tugs me out of the room.

"Let's give them some privacy," she says.

I lean against the corridor wall and let my head fall back. Closing my eyes, I sense despair rise within me. "What if they don't work it out? Everyone is coming to celebrate. What the hell are we going to do?"

What am *I* going to do if I see yet another relationship get burned to the ground?

"It's okay," Lucia soothes, rubbing her hands up and down my arm. "It's just one fight. They're stressed out and their tempers got the best of them, but they'll come around."

I groan and knock my head against the wall. "That's what I used to think about Mom and Dad, but eventually I realized they should never have been together in the first place."

"Take a breath," she says gently. "Couples disagree. Sometimes they even yell at each other. It doesn't mean their relationship is over."

I push away from the wall and pace across the corridor. "It doesn't mean they're okay either." Of course she wants to believe everything will work out. She still buys into the romance novel fantasy of happily ever after. "Be realistic. The world isn't sunshine and rainbows like in one of your books."

"Romance stories aren't all sunshine and rainbows." She sounds defensive. "They're a reflection of the fact that deep love is possible if people really want it and work hard for it." Her hands fist at her sides. When she notices them, she takes a breath and unclenches her fingers one by one. "Successful couples exist. They work through their problems. Your Mom and Kevin are upset right now, but if they truly care for each other, this will only be a blip on the radar."

I shake my head. She doesn't get it. Maybe they'll fix things temporarily, but how long before the next fight and the next? Before we know it, they'll be waging war over who gets the house and the car.

"I need some fresh air," I tell her. "I'm going to find a balcony."

She nods. "I'll come with you."

"No." The word is a little too forceful, and she flinches. "Sorry, sweetheart." I exhale slowly, knowing she shouldn't have to deal with my issues, no matter how frustrated I am. I'm being a dick. It's not her fault I'm upset or that I don't share her eternal optimism. I shouldn't have taken a swipe at her love of romance novels, especially knowing how sensitive she is about it. I bend to kiss her cheek. "I'm sorry," I repeat. "I'll just be a few minutes."

"Okay." She worries her lower lip with her teeth. "But you'll be back?"

I nod. "Soon."

I leave her in the hall. It's a jerk move, but I can feel my fears growing, and if I don't calm myself down, there's a chance I'll say worse than I already have. I'd never forgive myself if I did that. But as I let myself out an exterior door and feel the breeze on my skin, I can't help feeling like I've already lost her.

Chapter Ten

Lucia

Part of me wants to curl up when Tony leaves and make myself as small as possible. It bothers me that he took a cheap shot at something I love, but perhaps I should have been less Suzy Sunshine and just let him feel whatever he needed to. This can't be easy for him, especially when walking in on Gia and Kevin arguing must have brought up old memories for him and played into the fear that's been growing ever since they told him they were engaged.

I force myself to keep my shoulders back as I watch the corner Tony disappeared around. My instincts are screaming at me to go after him, but he needs space and I have to respect that. I linger in the corridor for a while, waiting for him to return, but when ten minutes pass and there's no sign of him, I duck back into the conference room. The yelling has stopped, and Gia stands alone. Her daughters have vanished—perhaps into the attached kitchen—and Kevin has retreated to the corner, where he's speaking quietly on his cell phone. Gia looks forlorn. She glances up when the door shuts behind me, and her expression becomes curious.

"Hi." I walk toward her slowly, not sure whether I'm overstepping by being here.

"Buongiorno," she says, her tone flat. "Can I help you?"

"I'm Lucia," I tell her. "I'm with Tony."

Pleasure flickers across her face but disappears quickly. "I'm sorry if you heard all that."

She swipes at moisture gathering beneath her eyes, careful not to smudge her mascara. Gia Romano is a good-looking woman. Her hair is long and dark with a healthy sheen that shows she takes care of herself. Her complexion is a shade warmer than Tony's, and she has rich brown eyes and full lips. I'd be willing to bet her daughters are as beautiful as Tony is handsome, with her genetics in play.

"I'm sorry for intruding," I say. "And I'm sorry you're having issues on what should be such a happy day."

"Pah." Gia shoots a glare at Kevin. "Some people don't value things the way they should."

"Perhaps," I allow, wondering how far I should go with this conversation. The smart thing to do would be to gracefully bow out and find Tony. But I've never been good at minding my own business, especially when it comes to couples in strife, and if writing a romance novel has taught me one thing, it's that problems can't be fixed unless people face them head-on. This might be Gia's relationship falling apart, but it impacts Tony, which means it involves me too. We need to discuss what's happening so all our stories can move forward. I take the plunge. "But isn't it sweet that Kevin just wants to marry you and doesn't care about any of the fancy trappings?"

Gia's eyes narrow. "I hadn't thought of it like that."

"Maybe you should," I suggest, knowing beyond a doubt I'm overstepping now, but holding on to my confidence that the intervention is necessary for her and I to both get our happily ever after. "And maybe you should also think about how seeing you fight publicly rather than trying to work together to resolve any problems affects your children."

Her demeanor turns cool. "What would you know about that?"

I take a couple of steadying breaths. "I know that Tony doesn't believe in happy long-term relationships because of all the divorces, breakups, and fights he's witnessed in this family."

She pales. "That can't be true." When I don't reply, she lays a hand on my arm. "Please, tell me it's not. Tony dates. Surely he wouldn't if what you've said is correct."

"When was the last time he introduced you to a partner?" I ask. When more color drains from her cheeks, I can tell she's realized I have a point. Tony might mention women to her, but I'd bet good money it's only in passing, to satisfy her curiosity.

"There have been none for years," she murmurs, more to herself than to me. "I can't believe I didn't see it." Her voice is heavy with shame.

"It's all right," I tell her. "It's not your fault your marriage ended or that he took it to heart. But if you think Kevin loves you and that what you have is worth salvaging, perhaps you should take the first step to make things right and show Tony that relationships are worth fighting for."

Gia looks me over from head to toe. "You're much wiser than you appear. Lucia is an Italian name, yes?"

"Yes," I agree. "My grandparents emigrated from Naples."

She nods and looks at me as though she sees right through me. It's unsettling, but I don't waver. "I think you'll be good for Tony," she says. "You're clearly willing to fight for him. Perhaps you are exactly what he needs."

Her unexpected praise makes my throat burn with emotion.

"I hope so," I whisper. But I'm afraid he'll never stop waiting for the other shoe to drop.

"For what it's worth, you have my blessing. It takes a brave woman to do what you just did." She steps back and our hands fall apart. "The party is on," she announces. "Excuse me. I need to talk to Kevin."

"Good luck." I slip out of the room again, hoping to find Tony in the corridor, but I don't see him among the people waiting to enter.

A woman in a hotel uniform is keeping them from going in. She glances at me as I leave. "Are they ready?"

"Probably soon," I reply. "But you'll want to check with Gia."

I move past the other guests and into the ladies' room. I need to hear a friendly voice. Someone who can help me make sense of things. I get my phone from my pocket and call Tempe. My sister-in-law answers quickly.

"Hi," I say. "Do you have a moment?"

"Of course." A wave of love for my new sister washes through me. "I thought you had that engagement party tonight?"

"I do, but there have been a few problems." I explain the situation to her. "You should have seen how much their fight freaked Tony out," I tell her. "Things have been really good between us, but after seeing how he reacted, I'm afraid he'll always have one foot out the door. He really believes that all relationships are doomed to fail."

"That's tough." She sounds sympathetic. "But it's still early days for you guys. He might come around."

"That's what I've been hoping for." But I also know I tend to be optimistic about most things. What if I'm waiting for something that won't happen? "I don't want to have my head in the sand like an ostrich and miss the signs that he's not as invested in our relationship as I am."

Tempe is quiet for a moment. I feel like I'm going to

climb out of my skin, waiting for her response. "I guess you'll just have to decide whether he's worth the risk."

I close my eyes. "He's worth everything, but I can't be the one who keeps reaching out."

"Then draw a line in the sand," she suggests.

"It's not that easy." But as I think about it, I realize it really is. I'll gladly risk my heart for Tony, but he had a scare tonight, and perhaps I need to leave it up to him to decide whether he wants to fight for our love. I can't do it for him. "Thanks, Tempe. That actually is helpful."

She wishes me luck, and we end the call.

I square my shoulders. Time to let the cards fall where they may.

———

Tony

I'm standing on a balcony that overlooks the street, gasping for air and trying to convince myself to go back inside, when the door opens behind me, and I hear footsteps approach. The clack of high heels tells me it's a woman, and I turn, expecting to see Lucia come to get me because I'm taking too long. I feel a pang of disappointment at the sight of Stella, but I suppress it and hope she doesn't notice.

"What's going on in there?" she asks, fishing in her purse for a cigarette and a lighter. "The guests are all waiting in the corridor, and when I tried to get into the conference room, the woman at the door stopped me."

"Mom and Kevin had a fight." My stomach churns at the memory. "I'm not sure if the party is going ahead."

"Huh." She places the cigarette between her lips and draws on it. "I definitely need this then." She blows a stream of smoke into the air. "Do you know what it was about? Mom has been high-strung lately. She wants everything to be just right, which is fair, but I think Kevin is overwhelmed by it."

"Something about a cake and a guest list and food requirements." I shake my head. "I'm not sure."

She winces. "Hopefully they sort it out soon, or people might start leaving." She glances around. "Speaking of people, where's your date?"

"Inside." Guilt rolls in my gut. "Waiting for me to come back."

"Oh, Tony." Her tone says, "you idiot." She's not wrong.

"I needed to get away for a while." Even as I defend myself, I know it's a losing battle. "I thought she'd come and find me if I took too long."

She takes another huff on the cigarette, the tip glowing. "Did you tell her you needed time alone?"

"Yes," I admit.

"Then why would she come after you?"

"I hate when you make sense." I guess I thought she'd see I was having second thoughts and want to reassure me. Now that she hasn't, I know it's all on me to make the next move. "It's just that seeing Mom and Kevin fight reminded me of how easily long-term relationships fall apart. How they never work out."

I expect Stella to agree. After her messy divorce, she surely shares my perspective. But to my surprise, she stares at me like I've said I like to eat dog shit in my spare time.

"Why the hell would you think that?" she asks, practically daring me to list the reasons.

"All of our family's marriages have fallen apart," I remind her. "Every last one. I would have thought you'd understand, given what you went through."

Stella drops her cigarette and stomps it under her heel. "Let me get this right. You think every relationship ends?"

"Well, yeah." I shrug, and there's a slight twinge in my shoulder.

She snorts. "You're a dumbass." She walks to the balustrade and rests her hands on the top rail, looking out over the traffic on the street below. "Every individual circumstance is different. None of our marriages worked, but that was for different reasons. And just like our relationships were different, others are different in that they don't end at all." She glances at me. "I'm not going to say that everyone who stays married is happy, but many of them are. There are also couples out there who choose not to marry but stay together for their entire lives. You can't just say 'relationships don't work.' The world isn't like that."

"But—"

The look in her eyes shuts me up.

"How much do you care for Lucia?"

I weigh the question. I already know I'm falling for her. I pause and imagine a life without her. It looks empty. Dull. My chest squeezes and my abdomen clenches unhappily. All of which tells me what should have been obvious. "I love her."

Stella's eyes twinkle. "Is being with her worth taking the risk that it might eventually fail?"

"Yes." I don't even have to think about it this time. She is absolutely worth the risk. "Excuse me, Stel. I need to grovel to my girlfriend."

"Good." She pats me on the back as I hurry to the door, but doesn't follow me into the hotel.

I retrace the steps I took earlier and find my way back to the conference room. Something significant must have happened since Stella joined me because there's no one in the corridor, and a cheerful hum buzzes beyond the door. I open it hesitantly and peer in. Dozens of people are mingling, smiling, and chatting. The tension from earlier is completely gone.

Mom and Kevin are holding court in the middle of the floor, and while I can see a hint of strain in the rigidity of Mom's back, she looks happy. She and Kevin have clearly made up. He's gazing at her the same way he did at my fight night—as though she's the center of his universe. I didn't understand that then, but I do now. I scan the room, searching for Lucia, and find her with Mia near the nibbles table. The two women seem to be getting along well, but something looks different about Lucia. I can't put my finger on it.

I square my shoulders and stride toward them. Lucia looks up as I approach, and our gazes lock. Mia is still speaking, but Lucia doesn't seem to hear what she's saying. Her attention is wholly on me.

"Mia, could you give us a moment to ourselves?" I ask as I reach them.

My sister's eyes narrow, but she must see something unusual in my expression because she nods and touches Lucia's arm. "I'll be back soon." To me, she hisses, "Fix whatever you did."

I bend to kiss Lucia's cheek. She doesn't make any move to reciprocate. Sweat breaks out on my palms, and I wipe them surreptitiously on my trousers. "I'm sorry," I tell her. "I shouldn't have snapped at you or left you like that. Especially when you didn't know anyone here and you already mentioned earlier that family events can be hard for you."

"You're right." She raises her chin and watches me steadily. I'm glad for the conversation around us because nobody seems to give us a second glance. "You shouldn't have. You knew that was a sore point for me, and while I understand why you needed a short time-out, you were gone nearly half an hour."

Shit. I hadn't realized it was that long.

"I apologize with all my heart, *tesoro*. Neither of those things will happen again."

Her spine loses some of its starch. "They'd better not. How are you doing now?"

"Much better. My sister talked some sense into me."

She cocks her head. "Which one?"

"Stella." I place my hands on her waist, hoping she won't pull away. She doesn't, but she holds herself distant. My heart thumps erratically. It's booming in my ears, and I'm amazed she can't hear it. "I'm sorry for being so on edge. I've realized I've been acting like it's a foregone conclusion that there'll come a day when I lose you. That might happen, but the only way it would be a certainty is if I never try to keep you in the first place." My fingers twitch on her waist, wanting to draw her closer. "I want to keep you, Lucia. I'm bound to screw up, but I'll do my best not to make the same mistake twice. You said romance novels are about working hard for your happy ending, and I'm prepared to do that, if you'll have me." I summon every last ounce of my courage. "I love you. *Ti amo*."

Her face softens, and she stretches up to capture my lips with her own. I breathe her in, relishing the taste of her. The scent of her. The feel of her body against mine. I'll do everything in my power not to give her up. "I love you too." She presses another kiss to my lips. "I want a future together. We'll have ups and downs, but I want to wake up and choose you every day. Will you do the same?"

"I will," I vow. "I'm going to read some of the books you like too. Will you tell me your favorites?"

"You don't have to do that."

"I want to give them a chance and to see why you love them so much."

Her mouth relaxes into a gentle smile. "Okay, then."

"So it's you and me?" I ask, not wanting to take anything for granted.

"You and me," she agrees, and I feel the rightness of it in my soul.

"Now, let me properly introduce you to my family."

Epilogue – 3 Months Later

Tony

Sweat drips from the tips of my hair as I execute the punch-kick combination Seth has called. His expression doesn't change as my strikes land on the pads. They're a bit weaker than they were pre-injury, but my technique is good, and best of all, there's no pain. The timer beeps, and he bumps his padded fist against mine.

"You're looking good." He nods approvingly. "I spoke to the P.T. this morning, and now that I've seen you myself, I agree with them. You're ready to return to training."

"Yes!" I pump my fist.

"But," he holds up a finger, "You have to build up slowly and let us know if you're hurting."

"I won't let you down." I can't hide a grin. It took me longer than I'd like to get to this point, but that's only because I'm impatient. As Lucia keeps telling me, I've recovered more quickly than many people would.

Seth slips the pads off and jerks a thumb toward the changing room. "Hit the showers. I want to see you back here tomorrow."

"You got it, coach." I remove my gloves as I head to

the lockers where my gear is stored. On the way, I pass several of my training buddies who bump my fist and welcome me back. Yeah, this is pretty damn perfect.

But I know something that will make it better.

I shower properly, taking the time to wash my hair, and dress in my best jeans and a collared shirt. Checking my watch, I see I'll be on time to pick Lucia up for our date. She doesn't know what I have in store, but I'm hoping she'll like it.

I leave the gym and drive to her place, where I park in the crowded lot and jog to her door. I knock and wait while she answers. When she does, lust thrums in my blood. It seems to never die around Lucia. I always want her. Constantly. Relentlessly. Especially when she's looking as drop-dead gorgeous as she does tonight, with a deep blue dress hugging her curves and bringing out the color of her eyes.

"Wow," I breathe when I remember how to think. "You look incredible."

"Thank you." She puckers her lips for a kiss, which I plant on her before guiding her out of the apartment. "Are you going to tell me where you're taking me?"

"Nope." I wink, enjoying the flash of chagrin that crosses her face. She's impatient, but she's also excited about the surprise. She loves when I do something special for her. "Trust me, sweetheart."

"I do."

We walk hand in hand to the car, and I instruct her to keep her eyes shut while I drive. When we arrive at the bar, I find a nearby parking spot.

"You can open your eyes now."

She blinks and her eyelashes flutter. She looks around and laughs. "Well, that was anticlimactic. I've got no idea where we are."

"Don't worry. I'm not going to let you down." I lock

my door and round the car to help her out. We walk half a block to the bar's entrance and wait while the bouncer checks her ID. He doesn't bother with mine, and I'm not sure whether to be insulted, but I let it go. Inside, groups of people are clustered around bar leaners. The overhead lights have a pink tinge, and the vibe is very eighties. I lead her to the only free table, glad I called ahead, so they haven't begun yet.

"Stay here," I tell her.

"Wait, you're leaving me?"

"Only for a couple of minutes." I kiss her cheek. "You'll see."

I thread between the tables and raise a hand at the bar to get the bartender's attention. When I tell him who I am and remind him we spoke earlier, he hands me a microphone.

"Good luck, man." He gestures to a woman in a glittery dress, who indicates for me to follow her to the small stage off to the side of the bar.

"I'll push a button in a couple of minutes," she says. "It will light up the stage and darken the rest of the bar. The music will start, and then you've got the floor. Are you ready?"

Nerves crowd in my stomach. "As much as I'll ever be."

"Great." She goes to the control panel, and I stand at the front of the stage.

When she hits that button, the rapid illumination startles me, and I nearly change my mind. But no, I'm doing this for Lucia. She deserves to live her dream. To be serenaded by someone who can actually sing.

And I *can* sing. It's not as though talent scouts are calling any time soon, but I have a nice voice. I sang in the church choir as a boy. Yes, I see the irony of a former choirboy becoming a playboy MMA fighter, but the playboy days are behind me now. The only woman I'm interested in is the one who's staring at me in shock. As the music starts, I grin at her and launch into my best rendition of "Time After Time."

At first, I'm conscious of the people watching, but as I reach the first chorus and Lucia raises a trembling hand to her mouth, everyone but her fades out of my vision. She's all I can see. All I'm aware of. The world consists only of Lucia and me as the lyrics wrap around us.

When the song ends, I hear applause but don't take my eyes off my woman. I place the microphone on the stage and jog over to her. She stands and throws herself into my arms.

"I can't believe you did that!" she cries. "Oh my God. You can sing." She pulls back, her eyes wide with excitement. "That was incredible."

"You liked it?"

"Uh, yes! That was the best thing anyone has ever done for me. I love you so much, Tony."

My lips tug up. "Enough that you'll move in with me?"

Her jaw drops. "Excuse me?"

Laughing, I pull her back into my arms and hug her tight. "I've been given the all clear to return to training, which means we aren't going to get to spend so much time together. I want to see you every morning and go to sleep holding you every night. Say you'll move in with me."

"I would love to." She practically bounces on her toes. "Especially now that I know you can sing. I want to be serenaded *every* night."

I shake my head, wondering what I've gotten myself into. "I suppose I can manage that. You'll get sick of it soon enough."

"No, I won't." Her expression grows serious. "I will never tire of you, Tony. I'll always want you around."

My heart seems to give an extra rat-a-tat-tat. "God, I love you. I'm so glad I get to be your happy ever after."

I press a kiss to her forehead and enjoy the way she feels in my arms, knowing I'll never tire of it either. With Lucia, everything in my life has an extra sparkle. One day, I'll make her my wife, and I don't feel any fear at the idea. Quite the contrary—I think that day will come sooner rather than later.

"You're mine, and I'm yours," she murmurs, then pulls away from me. "Wait here. It's my turn to serenade you."

I watch her go with a full heart, knowing she'll be back in my arms soon. Exactly where she belongs.

THE END

Fighter's Heart Excerpt

Lena

Eight words. That's all it takes to ruin my day.

"LaFontaine, I have a special assignment for you."

I recognize the voice without looking up from my desk. It's my prick of a boss, Adrian, and anything he's terming a "special assignment" will inevitably be a nightmare. That's all I get these days. The unfixable cases. The spoiled, self-entitled sports stars who screw up so badly, no one else wants them.

God, one massive win and I become the go-to public relations girl for the biggest jerks-with-abs in Vegas. Why can't I, just once, get a client who's a marginalized feminist with a cause? Sighing, I raise my head and meet Adrian's beady little eyes. This douchebag has my career in his hands, and he knows it.

"What's the case?"

His thin lips curl in a self-satisfied smile. It doesn't escape my notice that he's yet to close the door, which makes me wonder if he's keeping it open as an escape route.

"Jase Rawlins."

Oh. Hell. No.

"Nuh-uh," I say. "No freaking way."

Jase "The Wrangler" Rawlins is one of the bad boys of MMA. I don't even have to ask why he needs our services. Anyone who pays attention to the sports industry knows his ex-girlfriend has come forward with allegations of domestic abuse. I've seen photos of her bruised cheek and read the story in popular magazines. The guy is violent. But I suppose I shouldn't expect any different from a cage fighter.

I know the type. I've *dated* the type.

"There's no way I'm working with that asshole. Absolutely not. Find someone else. I'm not aiding and abetting a jackass who thinks he can get away with hitting women."

The door opens wider, and Jase Rawlins himself steps into my small, airy office, his gaze immediately drawn to the view out the window, which looks over the business district. I know him on sight, and I'm not even sorry he overheard my comment. He deserves all the condemnation he gets, and more. Fuck him.

Adrian's brows draw together, as if he didn't expect me to argue. "Everything is organized, Lena. The papers are signed. It's a done deal."

My teeth scrape together loud enough I'm surprised no one else hears them. I meet Jase's eyes, and a jolt runs through me. They're a strange color. Dark gray, or maybe green, it's hard to tell, and fringed with the thickest lashes I've ever seen. Pretty eyes. Out of place on a man known for choking his opponents into submission. He has high, arrogant cheekbones and plush lips, although the upper one is marred by a thin scar.

This is a face a woman could study forever—if she wasn't too caught up in his body. Because holy shit, he has a *body*. Broad shoulders, tapered hips, and strong legs with muscled calves showing beneath his shorts. Unfortunately, however panty-meltingly hot he is, he's also a brute, and I'm done with men like him. If I have anything to say about it, I'm not touching another MMA superstar—not with a ten-foot pole.

Time to shut this shit down.

"I'm *not* working with you," I tell him, and watch for a change in his expression, but his only reaction is a quick flick of his eyes to the right, where a man in an expensive suit has followed him into my office. "This is *not* a happening thing." I aim this comment at the suit, and he glowers. I don't care. There are some jobs even I won't take, and Adrian wants me to cross a moral line I'm not prepared to.

"Lena," Adrian says in a cautioning tone. "Hold on a moment."

Crossing my arms over my chest, I stare at him, wondering how far he's prepared to push. Considering Jase Rawlins is worth seven or eight figures, I'd hazard a guess that dollar signs are flashing in Adrian's eyes. Too bad. I don't operate that way. Money isn't my driver, and he knows it. So what approach will he take?

———

Jase

Sometimes, I wish it was legal to put someone in a chokehold outside of the cage. Like this uppity image specialist, for instance. Yeah, she may look like a schoolboy's wet dream in an ass-hugging pencil skirt and V-necked blouse, but it's obvious from the second she opens her mouth that she's already judged me and found me wanting. Nothing I'm not used to, but it still stings.

Maybe it's the fact my dick has some really great ideas about what he'd like to do with those gorgeous red lips, which are currently set in a sulky pout, or maybe it's her instant dismissal, but I want to rile her. To ruffle up her silky feathers and find out just how mouthy she can get.

I step forward before her boss can intervene, and raise a hand. As expected, everyone falls silent, which only seems to piss the redhead off more. Fuck, we haven't even gotten as far as exchanging names before she's mentally convicted me. That's the shitty part of being in the public spotlight. Everyone thinks they know me. They believe every stupid lie anyone tells.

Well, guess what? This girl doesn't know a goddamn thing.

"Calm down, cutie pie." I love it when her eyes chill to an icy blue, silently threatening to cut my balls off. Yeah, I knew she'd hate the pet name. Considering what she thinks of me, I don't give a crap. "Turns out, I don't want to work with you either." I raise a brow at Nick, my manager, and ask, "Is this really the best you could do?"

The redhead gasps, and I want to check whether she's crossed her arms tighter over her chest, plumping her little tits up, but I resist the urge to look.

"We can go somewhere else," Nick says. "I was told these guys are the best for miracles, but I'm sure we can find someone else just as good."

"Now, wait a minute," the stuffed shirt interjects. I wasn't listening when he introduced himself so I didn't catch his name. "Lena is the best there is. You won't find anyone else."

Finally, I succumb to the desire to glance at her and see how she's taking this. I catch the tail end of an eye-roll, and it makes me soften toward her a little. She's not drinking up the flattery the way some might.

Lena. I try her name out. It suits her. Pretty, bordering on pretentious but not overstepping the mark.

"Whatever puppy dog stunts *Lena*"—I emphasize her

name now that I know it—"wants to pull, they aren't going to do jack." I address Nick. "I still don't get why we're here. Give it a couple of days; Erin will decide she doesn't want to act on her threats, and the hubbub will die down."

Lena's face twists into a sneer. "Die down?" she demands. "The only way this shit-nado is dying down is if someone gets proactive about putting out your fires, and fast. Also, have a little respect for your girlfriend."

"*Ex*-girlfriend."

"Whatever." She says it like the "ex" part doesn't matter. As if Erin and I didn't break up more than two months ago now. "She's not some problem that will disappear if you ignore her. Domestic violence is a serious crime, and you can't just hand-wave it away." Her nose crinkles like she smells something bad. "It disgusts me that you're callous enough to think otherwise."

Callous? Me?

I count to five in my head and remind myself she doesn't know me. Her perception of me is based on what she's seen in the news, and I have to admit, it's damning. It also isn't true, but I don't bother saying that because this woman isn't going to believe me. Stuffing my hands in my pockets, I decide the best way to deal with her is to call her bluff.

"Okay, so you say the problem isn't going away on its own. What did you have in mind to fix it?"

"I… I…" She flounders, and I can't stop the smile that tugs at my lips. She's all bluster and no bite.

"That's what I thought." I turn to leave, but her smarmy boss lays a hand on my arm. When I stare at it, he snaps it back like he's been stung, his cheeks going pale. This guy is even worse than Lena. At least she has the balls to say what she thinks to my face. He's the type who'll pretend to be on my side, but all the while he's secretly fucking terrified of me.

"Wait, wait, wait," he says. "Give me two minutes to speak to Lena in private and talk her around. I promise you won't regret it."

Lena looks like she wants to bash him over the head with a paperweight, and I don't blame her. He's a condescending little shit. "Adrian—" she says.

"My office." He snaps his fingers, like he's ordering a dog to heel. "Now."

They leave, her trailing behind, practically dragging her feet, and Nick gives a low laugh. "Good old Jase. Always charming the ladies."

I jerk a thumb at the door. "Can we go? I've had enough of this."

He sighs, his expression regretful. "I wish we could, but what she said is true. Whether you want to believe it or not, this situation has the potential to derail your career."

"How can it, when I have the championship bout so soon? I'll blow Karson out of the water, and everything will be fine."

Nick ums and ahs. "That's if you don't get arrested before the fight."

"Pfft." I shake my head. "Not gonna happen. Erin is full of hot air."

"She also has a taste for the spotlight, and she'll keep spouting this bullshit as long as the cameras are rolling." Damn, he's right, and he must sense he has the winning hand because he powers on. "Not to mention, you promised Seth you'd take this seriously and do whatever you could not to tarnish the reputation of Crown MMA gym."

Ouch. Low blow. Nick knows I'd go to war for Seth if he asked. My trainer gave me everything. He had faith in me, took a chance on me, and he had no way of knowing I'd pan out to be a good investment. I was just a kid from a poor neighborhood with a mother of a chip on my shoulder and a willingness to shed blood to escape.

"Fine," I concede, not surprising either of us. "I'll hear them out."

But I have a bad feeling about this, and my gut doesn't often lie to me.

Acknowledgments

So, this novella wraps up all of my current stories in the Crown MMA Romance series and The Outsiders mini-series. As such, I want to give an extra special thank you to everyone who has been involved. In particular, Kate, for your support in editing. Donna, for proofreading and providing useful MMA term corrections thanks to your husband. Renita, for helping with sensitivity editing. Maria, for the wonderful covers. Thank you once again to my husband, family, and friends for your ongoing support, and to my readers, for coming on this journey with me and for being generally awesome.

Love you all.

Alexa

About the Author

Alexa (A.) Rivers writes romance with strong heroes and heroines who kick butt and take names. She loves MMA fighters, investigators, military men, bodyguards, and the protective guy next door who isn't afraid to fight the odds for love. She also writes small town romance as Alexa Rivers.